Praise for Nell Zink's

AVALON

"Well-observed, archly funny. . . . Zink is a brilliant creator of character, setting and, for lack of a better word, vibe, and there is much pleasure to be found in the way she gets so many things so precisely right in this novel."

—*San Francisco Chronicle*

"Zink is a fearless satirist. . . . Life steams ahead whether a person wants it to or not, and the mystery at work in *Avalon* is whether Bran is paranoid enough to realize that. Zink answers that question with her usual cunning, and it's no spoiler to note that the final page of the novel will send readers scrambling back to its first."

—*The Washington Post*

"[Zink] allows a remarkable tenderness to permeate the narrative, without compromising on her characteristic humor and predilection for the American idiom. The result is delightfully refreshing. . . . In the end, style and execution of that style are the skills with which the player wins the game, and Zink's knack for voice here is delicious."

—*Los Angeles Review of Books*

"*Avalon* contains delights. . . . [The novel's] discussions [are] lively and entertaining. . . . [Zink's] customary lunacy is on display again in *Avalon*." —*The Wall Street Journal*

"Incredibly pleasing . . . to see a writer this intelligent keep the focus of her gaze this tight. . . . There are also long stretches of satisfying narrative, of humanity and pain. . . . The concrete descriptions of California are continually stunning and add a further layer of life . . . [*Avalon*] ended up, for me, feeling like art."
—Lynn Steger Strong, *Los Angeles Times*

"Vivid and thorough—persistent, even, in its whimsy. . . . Zink writes, in places, with almost cinematic vividness, and follows Bran's evolution with an impressive commitment to realizing her experiences on the page."
—*Harper's Magazine*

"Zink delves into class, art, and American culture in a characteristically witty bildungsroman. . . . The style is all Zink's own, and she's as brilliant as ever here."
—*Publishers Weekly* (starred review)

Nell Zink

AVALON

Nell Zink left Southern California for eastern Virginia in 1972, aged eight. After completing a B.A. in philosophy at the College of William and Mary, she worked mostly as a secretary, with stints in masonry, technical writing, and translating. In 2000, she moved to Tübingen, Germany, and now lives near Berlin. Her books include *The Wallcreeper*, *Mislaid*, *Private Novelist*, *Nicotine*, and *Doxology*, and her writing has appeared in *n+1*, *Granta*, and *Harper's Magazine*.

AVALON

Avalon

NELL ZINK

Vintage Books
A Division of Penguin Random House LLC
New York

FIRST VINTAGE BOOKS EDITION 2023

All rights reserved. Published in the United States
by Vintage Books, a division of Penguin Random House LLC,
New York, and distributed in Canada by Penguin Random House
Canada Limited, Toronto. Originally published in hardcover
in the United States by Alfred A. Knopf, a division of Penguin
Random House LLC, New York, in 2022.

Vintage and colophon are registered
trademarks of Penguin Random House LLC.

The Library of Congress has cataloged the Knopf edition as follows:
Name: Zink, Nell, author.
Title: Avalon / Nell Zink.
Description: First edition. | New York : Alfred A. Knopf, 2022.
Identifiers: LCCN 2021040949
Subjects: LCGFT: Novels.
Classification: LCC PS3626.I55 A95 2022 | DDC 813/.6—dc23
LC record available at https://lccn.loc.gov/2021040949

Vintage Books Trade Paperback ISBN: 978-0-593-46815-9
eBook ISBN: 978-0-593-53490-8

Book design by Maria Carella

vintagebooks.com

Printed in the United States of America
10 9 8 7 6 5 4 3 2 1

AVALON

CHAPTER ONE

I lay on my backpack, denying to myself that my arm was broken. The moon had made me think it was light enough to gambol down a mountain. The waterfall meadow, the tissue-paper leaves, the iceberg clouds and diamond rocks, the moon a puddle of dead frogs: looking down from the front steps, I had seen the world in shades of white. But it was black, a soft mix of hairlike grass and crumbly dirt that held me aloft, poised between Earth's molten core and outer space, while I ran my fingers up and down my arm.

I sat upright. A smear of moonlight led to the Isle of Avalon. But there was no island, and my arm was fine. The more I kept probing around, the more okay it felt.

The night was warm. I took off my backpack and leaned back on my hands, looking up and out at the torn black firmament strewn with airplanes. The wind picked up and long grass tickled my face. I wondered whether my car would start. I heard a big dog snuffling, and Peter's voice saying, "Whoa, slow down, Rabelais!"

He was coming closer. He had something more to say to me.

He stopped about ten feet behind me. I could hear by the scrabbling that he was holding the dog by its collar. He waited, but I could not look at him.

Softly he said, "Guess what? She called first and told me to go to hell." He paused. "What a fucking disaster. I don't know who told her, but now there's nothing . . ." He paused. "Nothing to keep us apart but this damn dog."

The stars blurred with inexpressible happiness. Why would they do that? Is there any possible ethical justification?

Avalon means "place with apples," the healthy food that grows on trees. If you take good care of apples, they stay fresh all year. That's why Arthur was taken to Avalon to heal his wounds.

On Easter Sunday 2005, when I was in fourth grade, my mother and common-law stepfather, Doug, took me there with my common-law stepbrother, Axel. The passenger ferry sailed from Long Beach, California, south of L.A. Whoever named the tourist-trap town on Santa Catalina Island "Avalon" presumably hoped to benefit from the marketing cachet of King Arthur while evoking such additional mythical Western island paradises as Tír na nÓg, Emain Ablach, and Atlantis. "Avalon's where Arthur lives," my mother shouted, pointing at it and adding, "He's not real." Her world had a real-life king, the Dalai Lama. The ship plowed through low swells, steady as a train. Tormented seagulls tormented my ears with cries of torment, demanding French fries I did not have and would not have wanted to give up. Walleyed, impassive flying fish spoke their silent greetings—patently magical beings, stiff and papery as they outpaced the ship, Arthur's scaly heralds.

In Avalon, we rode in a glass-bottomed boat and saw wild goldfish. Then we ate burgers from an open-air stand. I was having a phase where I only wanted the patty with nothing on it, so Axel ate my bun. Catalina also has bison and antelopes, but we never set foot past the harbor.

Not long after our trip, my mother moved to a Tibetan Buddhist monastery, leaving me alone with Doug and his family. I still have the books she left behind: *The Once and Future King. The Crystal Cave. The High King.* She also left a bunch of Tolkien, but Doug sold it.

I have trouble recounting my childhood in chronological order. It appears in fragments, like a cored and sectioned apple. Put it back together, and the interior disappears. My earliest firsthand memory is of the soft feel of the long rectangle of dust behind an inch-thick steel plate—the kind they use to cover holes during road construction, about four feet on a side, with two round holes so a crane can pick it up—that leans against the cinder-block wall of a fertilizer shed at Bourdon Farms. The strange hush back there, the oblique light, the sharp odor. Under my pinkish-yellowish right hand, the littering of cement and rust untouched by irrigation or rain. I know I was almost a baby, because the steel plate is still there and the space behind it is tiny. Was I playing, or hiding, or both? I have no idea. The preponderance of my information is secondhand.

The Hendersons of Torrance, California, run a business that has been passed down through generations. Their house is filled with clan memorabilia, and so is the yard. A historic freezer, door still attached, contains a mildewed baseball bat decorated with Aztec temple scenes in a combination of wood-burning and enamel paint. A shallow well run dry contains a broken rocking chair with a handworked needlepoint seat. Doug once tried to use it as a sled on mud after a rain. It worked enough to try once, he told me, and then he threw it in the well. In childhood I turned the crisp black pages of green photo albums, recognizing our front porch behind a white-haired man at the wheel of a familiar 1920 Model T Ford. Long decommissioned, it stank of chickenshit. There had been no chickens in my lifetime.

The property is six-plus acres under the high-tension lines that run from La Fresa down to Redondo Beach. It stretches from road to ravine to road, with fences maintained by the power company, the perimeter traced by a dirt-bike trail where Grandpa Larry once ran races with his biker-barfly best friends. The business is a plant nursery specializing in exotic imports and topiary. In 1978, California Proposition 13 limited local property taxes to one percent of a home's 1976 assessment. Moves, additions, and new construction triggered punishing reassessments. To maintain conspicuous consumption while living in the same modest houses for fifty years, rich people took up gardening. That was where Bourdon Farms came in.

Whether anything other than tropical plants ever arrives in those shipping containers bound to the port of Long Beach, and whether the Hendersons' motorcycling friends have anything to do with distributing it, I do not know. I was never considered a member of the family unless they wanted something from me.

As with many family businesses, the key to the enterprise's viability is unpaid labor by women, children, and recent immigrants in need of a place to lie down. At best, gray market; more likely, black. But revenuers do not fuck with the Hendersons. It would take the FBI, and it would take years. A simple search would turn up nothing. Nobody keeps the books or deposits money in the bank. They would apologize to the feds for knowing nothing (they reject federal authority on principle) and refer them to their imaginary absentee employer, Mr. Bourdon.

The land is on California's statewide property inventory. I know that much. I figured it out using the internet at my high school—that the land belongs to the state. I asked Doug about it. He told me that Great-Great-Grandpa Allan's ranch stretched for miles, all the way to the Madrona wetlands, where he watered his cattle. The state condemned it by eminent domain to build the city of Torrance, compensating his heirs with an exemption from all applicable law in perpetuity. "That's why we fly the flag of the California Republic," he explained, referring to the state flag with its grizzly bear and red star. "It's the one place left where a man can stand tall."

The house is an Appalachian-style Cape Cod with vinyl siding and a tin roof, hunched on brick pillars over a low crawl space. Except for the TVs, which are always state-of-the-art, the furniture is an unchanging assortment of beat-up antiques, compounding the difficulty of sorting memories into epochs without using my own size as a reference.

Grandpa Larry occupied the master bedroom. At age two and a half I switched from sharing an upstairs room with Mom and Doug to sharing one with Axel. When I was six, I took over the unheated lean-to, which reeked of mice, outside what was once the back door. The lean-to had been added before the vinyl siding was put on, so my walls were made of pine and I could use thumbtacks to post pictures cut out of magazines. I had two doors and a tiny window that could not be opened.

The bikers maintained a clubhouse on the property, over which the California bear and a black POW/MIA flag flew day and night. When they were drunkest, they would sing "He Ain't Heavy, He's My Brother." They consciously maximized eating and smoking, equating size and rugged looks with masculinity. I am certain that in their minds no real man was ever naked. Identity was a question of tools, machines, leathers, and weapons. They were trans-human cyborgs.

The laborers were nicer. The foreign songs they taught me are gone, but I remember all their names—Eric, Roger, and sometimes Simon—because Grandpa Larry was a one-man Ellis Island from hell. New York immigration authorities a hundred years prior had assigned immigrants Anglo names, and Grandpa Larry approved. Each Eric was replaced with an Eric and each Roger with a Roger, so that the nursery was consistently staffed with one of each, Simon being optional for the Easter and Christmas rush. The Hendersons fed them, housed them, invited them to watch TV in their home—although they were not welcome to use our bathroom—gave them work, failed to pay them, and let them know they were free to move on at any time.

They typically stayed for under one month. They had their own shack with propane-heated water on demand, sharing our illegal septic tank. Their shower setup was designed for horse barns off the grid and not for human residential use, but they seemed to like being off the grid. Once (I was about fourteen) I helped Doug take a Norfolk Island pine over to Rancho Palos Verdes and we ran into a guy from Burkina Faso who had stayed with us for maybe two weeks the year before. He had a team leader job with an expensive lawn-care service and was going by the name Roger Bourdon.

———

I started work at age three, gathering snails in a bucket and lugging them to West 190th Street to be run over. This was because my mother wanted Bourdon Farms to stop using snail bait. She liked cats. The strays she fed were constantly dying of metaldehyde poisoning. They were replaced by new strays, which also died horribly. The management, however, saw my work as complementary to snail bait, not as a substitute.

Mom was never allowed up on the backhoe or the forklift, but by the time she left, she could repot, wrap root balls, and prune. On Sundays, our day of rest, she would strap me into the passenger seat of Doug's truck and drive the PCH (the Pacific Coast Highway that ran near our house) north past Will Rogers Beach to cut back via Sunset Boulevard, always detouring to a street in Brentwood that was lined with banyans. She would roll slowly through the arcade of columnar prop roots, gazing admiringly on the wealth represented by big trees that crowded the road like a jungle straining at the leash. Then we would sit for a while under the gigantic Moreton Bay fig (my suspicion is that it started life—I mean Mom's inner life—as Yggdrasil and become the Bodhi tree) at a Presbyterian church near Palms and Sepulveda, waiting for the service to end so we could scam food and beverages from their buffet before taking the freeway home.

When I try to remember best what she was like, I think of her on the long drive back to Torrance, wordlessly and willfully happy, with the window down and her hair tousled by the wind. Which is strange and kind of sad, because I was there the whole time—her own child, staring in parallel with her out the windshield, afraid to break her concentration.

There was a Buddhist center in Pacific Palisades that was the prettiest house on Sunset. Maybe that was what did it. It might have been the traffic. We would be trapped somewhere, barely moving, and she would tell me to pretend this moment was the only thing that had ever happened and would ever happen in my life and that it was eternal, and to ask myself whether life would still be worth living. She started buying magazines with pictures of all different lamas and bodhisattvas in them and sneaking away to meditate. After nine years with Doug, she took off to a Buddhist center in the Sierras, with whopping trees galore, and became a nun.

Her parents, Grandma Tessa and Grandpa Lamont, were fond of me, but they lacked resources. Grandpa Lamont had been diagnosed as mentally retarded in childhood and housed in state institutions until he was drafted and the army discovered that he had treatable petit mal epilepsy. Grandma Tessa had been a seamstress for Bell Helicopter in Fort Worth. They met at a Masonic convention in Chicago and moved together to Pasadena to set up a debt-powered business leasing copiers to storefronts, and when I was a child they were broke. As far as I know, their biggest extravagance was my annual trip to Knott's Berry Farm, once a year from ages six to thirteen. Their poverty denied me the American Jerusalem (Disneyland—Disney World in Florida being the Mecca). They lived in a single-wide in a seniors-only mobile-home park. When Mom left, they took me in for eight days, from a Saturday to the following Sunday. No one under fifty-five was allowed to stay there more than a week. They had to pay a fifty-dollar fine for keeping me an extra day.

The Hendersons were happy to keep me on. A ten-year-old stepchild represented circa eight years of unpaid labor and a potential twenty thousand dollars in earned income tax credits, if the IRS played along. From their perspective, my mother offered me to them in payment for her freedom.

Freedom from what? From raising me? From being around me? That was what I thought, because she never came to visit, or asked for me back. A monastery in Tibet would have taken a ten-year-old, and even in California it could have been passed off as home schooling, but her place was adults-only. It was old school Tantric—Nyingma—with red robes, a golden stupa, big statues, rock gardens, incense, prayer wheels, mantra chanting, sand paintings, whatever else, and the whole nine yards. The site was a former motel on the road from Fresno to Yosemite, hidden on an incline behind fir trees. To the first-time visitor it looked kind of amusing, because the lobby had been built in the shape of a wigwam.

Mom worked there in exchange for room and board, as she had at Bourdon Farms. But she got a better deal. The Buddhists did not pressure her to work hard or fast, and they gave her free time to meditate.

Their central practice was the cultivation of conscious awareness of every tiniest movement and nerve impulse, which could be combined with all kinds of unskilled labor, such as vacuuming the pool. A person who slows down enough will hallucinate a ghostly presence to take up the perceptual slack. In her case it was a blue orb behind her left shoulder.

Doug took me to see her twice, when I was twelve and

fifteen. Both times she never stopped smiling. The first time, she was very thin. The second time, she looked so hungry that I gave her the hard-boiled eggs from my bag lunch. She was allowed to eat animals if someone else killed them, and the eggs had never lived, strictly speaking. She told me she was happy and how much she loved me, the recruits she trained, her fellow monks and nuns, and her Rinpoche.

When I lay in bed obsessing about her after my visits, the orb always bugged me. If the point was to cultivate minute consciousness awareness, how was it helping?

Later it turned out she had ovarian cancer the whole time. But when she wasn't scrubbing toilets or raking pine needles with maximum mindfulness, she was silently meditating to take her mind off reality, so that nobody noticed until it metastasized to her back and she couldn't work.

She died at the monastery with whatever palliative medicine Medicaid gives nuns. I cried with single-minded attention and felt her presence as a vague epiphenomenon to my rear, like the orb but yellow. Maybe because she had blond hair when I was little.

Then Doug took her back. He stormed up to Oakhurst in a hearse with an undertaker from Gardena to secure her valuables and save her remains from the heathens he claimed would have fed her to condors on a charnel ground. He had her cremated "like a normal person" and took me along to scatter the ashes in the duck pond at the park in Manhattan Beach where, he told me, they had shared their first kiss after club sandwiches and coffee at the Kettle on a cloudy summer afternoon three years before my father's emigration had prompted him to leave Axel's mother for mine.

That was the first I had heard of my father's emigration. I was sixteen. I was like, "What?"

According to Doug, my father moved to Australia when I was eleven months old. My mother was still on maternity leave from her job at the yogurt factory where my father was a supervisor, because I screamed so much, ate so slowly, and had trouble keeping things down.

My father planned the move as a surprise. He sold his parents' former home in Hollywood out from under us and leased a one-bedroom apartment on West 190th in Torrance. He paid a year's rent up front and gave Mom enough cash to hold out for a year.

To my mom, Torrance was West BF, convenient to nothing unless you counted the tar-studded municipal beach where she first saw Doug. Trash bags on hoops whipped emptily in the wind while seniors fought heart disease with wrist and ankle weights in the shade of chemical potties. The contrast had made Doug look good, but not good enough, which irritated him. For the remainder of her marriage, he gave her no peace.

Dad stayed at the Torrance apartment for two nights. Then he caught a plane to a place where he could realize his life's dream. His life's dream was to be single again, marry a faithful woman, have different children, pay us nothing, and ignore us, his parents, and his sister forever. After Dad left, Doug convinced Mom to give him the cash, sublet the apartment, and move to Bourdon Farms.

———

I was neither physically molested nor abused by the Hendersons. By the time I started kindergarten, Grandpa Larry was making speeches about how he would castrate any male who touched me. The speeches bothered my mother, but not enough for her to contradict him. Sometimes Doug and Axel chased me as if we were playing tag, daring Grandpa Larry to cut off their balls. But they and the laborers kept their distance, and so did Grandpa Larry, so that in a certain almost entirely imperceptible sense, I had a sheltered upbringing. I was never bullied at school. Axel was three years older and widely reputed to have beaten an injured coyote to death with a bicycle lock.

They had no plans for me, other than to keep me busy.

Working on motorcycles will do that to you: they could not differentiate between having fun and creating the conditions for it. Enjoyment was their assigned task, duty, and role in life. It required enablement through labor, sometimes their own. My work, no different from their motorcycle maintenance, contributed to their enjoyment. They drew no emotional distinction between asking me to wash fungicide residues off a shipment of "organic" palmettos, leaf by knifelike leaf, and pounding a six-pack in preparation for a race. Both were necessary steps in their enjoyment.

I ate every scrap of food that was put in front of me. It was never too much. We had two refrigerators stocked with beer, but no working oven in the house. The one my mother used had become involved in a grease fire that damaged the electronics. We used it to store bread safe from rodents. The adults subsisted on USDA Prime beef that "fell off a truck." Axel and I shared canned foods warmed with propane. If the timing was right we could exploit the adults' mesquite charcoal to eat straight from the can like cowboys—SpaghettiOs, corned-beef hash, baked beans, refried beans, Spam. I learned to wrap potatoes, frozen burritos, frozen pizzas, and the like in foil and nestle them in the coals.

But either the cans and burritos and pizzas were smaller than they had been in Doug's childhood (he did the shopping), or Axel was hungrier than Doug had ever been, because I became a gaunt, leggy child with limbs like sticks, who ate scraps off plates before doing the dishes.

I completed as much homework as I could fit into the minutes between my arrival at school in the morning and the opening bell, and my grades were okay. I wolfed down my free school meals while studying my textbooks. Teachers tried to interest me in extracurricular activities, but I was due home every afternoon to help in the nursery until nightfall.

With each day of encroaching puberty and its attendant increase in self-awareness, I became more miserable. I cried in bed, afraid of recurring nightmares in which I saw my mother die, always in banal situations. She would collapse on the floor of a public restroom or choke on a walnut. To counteract my dreams, I fantasized an orchard paradise full of flowers, and kindly kidnappers who wrapped me in an area rug and stowed me in an intermodal shipping container to take me there.

These were not sexual fantasies. Their essence was escape.

In the hours that prefaced the crying and the fantasies, I reread my mother's high-fantasy novels, identifying sometimes with plucky heroes and princesses, more often with service animals such as Taran's horse Melynlas—though I was young yet to gild duress by couching my service as willing—but mostly with entire realms threatened by advancing darkness. I identified with the world. The main character in all those books is the world in trouble, and it was me.

When the school counselor hesitantly asked, in fifth grade, whether I had thoughts about harming myself (my arms and legs were all scratched up from work), I thought: What a crazy question! Myself, of all people? Is she blind? I frowned and said, "No!" Now I know that the Hendersons had a reputation that made others tiptoe around them. People ascribed responsibility for their actions—framed as reactions—to virtually anybody but them, and dismissed my abortive attempts at complaint as guilty whining.

CHAPTER TWO

Two years after my mother's departure, there materialized a child willing to talk to me. I paused to look at the pinup of Camarón de la Isla inside his locker door, he said he liked my lumberjack shirt, and from thenceforth we saw each other nearly every day. Not that having a friend was quite enough to save me. But it helped.

He was a year ahead—in seventh grade when I was in sixth—so at first we conversed only in snippets over our cafeteria lunches. By summer we were sharing every experience we could, resolutely bound to each other. We were both determined to see our lives witnessed, though our commentary remained superficial and beside the point, as befits children.

His name was Jay and he was a pariah. His parents brokered commercial real estate, working long hours to earn humongous windfalls at odd intervals. They had adopted him from Russia as a baby and placed him in the care of a nanny. From what he said, they were no longer sure his adoption had been a good idea. But his changeling status in the family offered a signal advantage: he was under far less pressure to be like his dad than your typical sole male heir.

The Hendersons and the laborers saw he was gay the

moment he first arrived home with me, five months into our friendship. He had worn flamenco boots to school—boots for which he had whined to his parents for a long time—and bullies had thrown them down a storm drain.

He was the kind of slightly-built kid who should carry a skateboard for self-defense, not be rocking two-inch slanted heels. Vaguely Central Asian cheekbones and ethereally fine chestnut hair only heightened the fey look that drew bullies to him like flies to sherbet.

His parents had plenty of money to buy him more goofy boots. They were so liberal and tolerant, they even sent him to public school to rub shoulders with the hoi polloi. In refusing him the boots, they had merely hoped to save him from himself.

But he did not want to be socially accepted. He wanted to be unique. Not because he hoped to get away with it in middle school—he was not that dumb—but because an inchoate pubescent longing urged him to inspire outside intervention through performative suffering. The boots were self-harm.

Still, he felt he could not face his nanny, Mrs. Imai, and the domestic staff in sock feet, so he had walked me home in hopes of borrowing shoes of some kind.

I was growing and all my shoes were too small, even for me, so I lent him a pair of plastic zoris. Then I had to work. He helped me clip all the brown bits off an order of near-rootless tree ferns set for delivery to an indoor mall. A Roger who was transporting liquid fertilizer in a plastic tank with a forklift throttled his engine and said amiably, "Who's your punk?"

Jay answered, "I'm nobody's punk!"

Roger called out, "Come on, Bran! Tell us, Bran! Who's your punk, Bran?" He put the forklift back in gear and was soon out of earshot. "Bran" is short for "Brandy."

"You're not a punk," I said. "You're the only normal person I know." It took me until I was sixteen to figure out that he would never marry me.

Twice a week, Mrs. Imai drove him to a studio in Venice Beach for private dancing lessons with an old hippie lady named Loretta who had spent half her life in Seville. She could legally drive with a telescopic lens that corrected one eye to 20/200. After lessons, she took him out for ice cream. A few times, she even drove him home, but only until he told his parents she was blind. After that, Mrs. Imai waited for him.

I learned a lot from Loretta, even though I met her only a few times. The correct posture for flamenco is *sentada,* sitting while standing up. In every position you keep your elbows as high as they will go, and your hands (for girls) never stop circling. She danced with a weird glamour and a limited range of motion, in red leotards that emphasized her ribs and long ruffled skirts that hid her legs, her white hair woven into a crown with bobby pins and surmounted by a comb.

She wore high-heeled ankle-strap shoes. Grandma Tessa told me that whores wear ankle-strap shoes for safety, never going barefoot even in bed, while respectable women wear pumps they can kick off at will in a carefree and liberated manner. But it was already plain to me, even without the explanation, that the point of dance outfits was to look contemptible standing still and command respect only by dancing. Costumes were a time-honored method of coercing people to perform, so that there would be something to watch before the invention of TV.

Jay was a supremely untalented dancer. It is hard to describe, as a friend, how he looked when he danced. Imagine a pedophile who is a serial killer of puppies on the side but willing to spare a few in exchange for sex with Jay. Jay hears the offer while directing traffic. The threat casts him backward like a gust of wind, face twitching with emotion, heels pounding the rhythm of a temper tantrum as he bargains with fate. Circling it seductively, he conveys vulnerability, weakness, and the unmistakable message "Let me evacuate my bowels first." I mean, no joke, it was that egregious. Flamenco tore the mask off the controlled routine of his schoolboy existence, and what it revealed was not good. Or it was good, being an authentic part of Jay, but no more made for exposure than his gallbladder or hypothalamus. Only by shutting my eyes could I nullify the critical voice of the advancing darkness we look to for salvation, which was also my voice.

As Jay's eighth-grade year drew to a close, it became apparent that he would be leaving me to go to high school. I demanded to skip eighth grade so we could stay together.

Unbureaucratic by nature, tradition, habit, and reputation, Grandpa Larry visited the principal's office and enlisted me in the Class of 2012. If school was a waste of time, I might as well get it out of the way fast—that was his thinking. What the school thought made no difference to anyone, even the school.

At West High, Jay and I were suddenly no longer conspicuous. Pressure to conform increases in adolescence, while individual capacity declines. Social anxiety becomes the norm. To stand out, it was enough to be neither Japanese nor Korean. We acquired friends. To be more precise, my adored Jay instantly fell in love with a comely, bone-straight boy named Henry. In the chaotic opening weeks of ninth grade, establishing contact with him across the social divide we thought separated us turned out not to be an insurmountable challenge. By the time we figured out we were fellow untouchables, we were hardworking members of his staff on the school's literary magazine.

Henry tanned dark and had curly hair that turned reddish in summer. His family had been Okies who fled the Dust Bowl and risen to own an RV dealership, and his ambitions involved business. There was open speculation about "what" they might be. His big brother had gotten a DNA test that said they were part North African, but there was no consensus on whether that made him African-American. He thought it did. He was handsome in a square-jawed, muscular way, an excellent student, and could play the trumpet and swim butterfly. A former Boy Scout, he volunteered with the Red Cross. But he was considered a misfit, eligible for friendship with the likes of Jay and me, because he was dating Fifi. They had been together for so long—a hand-holding child romance that had turned into a sexual thing so early it was illegal—that they acted like an old married couple, role-playing and bickering to change it up. They had loud fights, even at school. Their maturity made teachers nervous.

Fifi's mother was a Nikkei CAD operator, and her father a Black dentist from Atlanta. She had a dark Asian face and wavy hair, and she loved all things fuzzy, such as corduroy, velour, chenille, and acrylic tights in bright colors under skirts—that is, she dressed like a toddler and was conspicuous everywhere she went. Everything about her was rounded, from her surprised-looking eyes (opening them wide was her way of noting other people's impossible behavior, and she did it a lot) to her tiny feet. The family's house was furnished Japanese-style and their summer vacations were spent in Japan, but as tourists, because her Japanese relatives had stopped talking to her mother before her older brother was born. He identified as Japanese. He wanted to take their mother's name and reunite the extended family. Possibly it was a standard-issue sibling-rivalry-motivated division of labor, but his bridge-building mania—trying to force his mother to speak Japanese with him and the Japanese kids at school to accept him and so on, as if a bridge could close a rift—spawned nonstop public embarrassment. Fifi distanced herself from such scenes at an early age, emerging with a hair-trigger intolerance of conflict.

She identified with her relatives in Atlanta. In her mind she was a Black Georgian, relaxed, polite, and pragmatic, and woe to those who dared be otherwise. The consensus at school was "such a bitch."

She studied like a demon to assure herself perfect grades and test scores, because she wanted to top her father's career by becoming a Black orthodontist with billionaire patients. But she worked in his dental practice after school and had no time for philanthropy or sports. Henry planned to attend UCLA, and she planned to go along. To ensure her acceptance, her transcript had urgent need of an extracurricular activity.

The social-outcast power couple pounced on the school's dead-in-the-water literary magazine. For three years before they revived it, it had placed staff photos in the yearbook without actually putting out an issue. The unused budget had piled up to a substantial sum, because no one cared enough even to embezzle the money.

Staff positions were assigned according to need. Henry became executive editor so he could meet rich people—his future clients, perhaps the grandparents of Fifi's future patients—while soliciting advertising. Fifi became editor in chief because she needed leadership positions for her college applications. Jay became poetry editor because he wanted to go to college with Henry and Fifi. My role was to be Fifi's assistant, reading submissions, for which she had no time. Our other friend, Will, did layout and graphics and maintained our online presence.

Will had no need of the magazine. He had such good test scores that he might get in anywhere he applied. Like several of our fellow pupils, he had attended our inaugural staff meeting because he needed more extracurricular activity on his record, but unlike the others, he stayed longer than one minute. He had gone to elementary and middle school with Jay and me without our ever exchanging a word. As a little boy he was considered quite cool for the casual flair with which he mastered various video games, before his profound beauty challenges landed him with us. Will battled cystic acne with drugs that required him to wear shiny sunblock indoors. He had a narrow face with a receding chin and protruding front teeth that made him look, at best, thoughtful.

His parents were Jewish and his look, he claimed, was "Asian nerd" because—he claimed—Jews are Asians. It was the worst brand of geek irony, offensive, yet opaque, based on an old fascist idea that Jews are "Orientals." Possibly the joke was his own and not cribbed from some online forum. It was hard to know what he was capable of thinking. He talked so little compared to the others. He talked barely more than I did.

Submissions consisted largely of fan-fictional musings

about the sex lives of TV and movie characters submitted by an older (as in possibly twenty—he had been held back twice or three times in elementary school for truancy) Cuban guy who wore silk bomber jackets and had a crush on Henry. A certain amount was trash by pranksters hoping to upset Fifi and set her off in public for entertainment purposes. But every quarter, like clockwork, students with academic or literary aspirations submitted earnest poems and stories modeled on those in the Common Core, and we published them. Every year under Henry's management, we won awards for public high school literary-magazine excellence.

In ninth grade, we had not yet formed a clique. We met only once a week, during professional-development period in the school library. There were few other patrons, and the part-time librarian, a retiree in her seventies, seldom left her office. Multiple intervening barriers stood between me and my home—my fellow editorial staff members, dense walls of books, the thick steel doors of the school, its walled compound, the drug-free school zone—and I had a role to play, occasionally speaking up to say, "That was okay" or "That one sucked." At those meetings I was the happiest I had ever been in my life.

The following July, Will crept over to Bourdon Farms on a dare (from Jay) to get a look at Grandpa Larry, who immediately demanded to be shown his circumcised penis, playing at the idea that Jews were of interest to science. Never taking his eyes off the TV, Grandpa Larry fiddled at his own fly while a blonde with blurred red lips read the evening's headlines from a teleprompter and he described her blow job technique down to the last iota. Eric and Roger (Christians) got up and left.

It was all an elaborate joke, but we and the laborers had "no sense of humor." Grandpa Larry used creepiness the way other people use charisma, to dominate a room.

The event produced an excellent and ultimately life-changing outcome, which was that Will issued a standing invitation for me to come over to his house whenever I wanted. The Grandpa Larry experience had educated him, making him nicer. I never once heard him make another joke designed to be somehow so offensive it was funny.

The new friendliness was not because he "liked" me. He never tried to speak to me alone. He claimed to like all the same "hot" girls all the boys liked. We were not close. But I started visiting on Sundays anyway, often finding Jay there, and sometimes Henry and Fifi as well.

By the middle of sophomore year, the magazine was head-quartered at Will's place, which made sense. It had better computer equipment than the school. We worked on layout in his bedroom and held editorial meetings in the living room.

The house wasn't huge like Jay's, but it was cozy. We were underfoot there, and his parents could not possibly ignore us—we were loud—but they never tried. They seemed to enjoy young people, so much that it seemed odd to me that Will had no siblings. Instead, they had an Old English sheepdog named Lionel, who was bathed and brushed and allowed on all the furniture, like a living throw blanket.

Will's mother, Susan, taught me to cook. I was curious, wanting to know where tasty food came from, and she was nice enough to show me. She smiled patiently while I lauded her most delectable creations, such as grilled cheese sandwiches made with natural Cheddar and non-rancid butter.

She was a pediatrician. She routinely wore wrap dresses and leather-soled shoes and kept her hair smooth as glass. I thought she looked ready to go on TV. Will's father, Mark, was a public defender who wore suits on trial days and kicked back on weekends by taking off his tie.

Myself aside, everyone in our clique had two healthy parents who were married to each other. I thought they were normal and I was not, if only because lucky people are the minority that establish the norms behind the concept of normality.

My love for Jay endured until I got drunk at his house the Saturday after my sixteenth birthday and woke up with a neat set of bite marks on my left upper arm. He said we had been watching TV, and I wouldn't stop laying my arm on the sofa cushion behind his head no matter how he flinched, so he turned around and bit it hard, right through the flannel.

I told him how I felt. He responded with kindness, explaining that being gay involves failure to be straight. We could have sex, he said, because he was so horny all the time, but he would not fall in love with me. He would make me unhappy, guaranteed. Then he hugged me, because he had made himself feel safe.

My feelings for him had little to do with sex, which to my mind was nothing to be proud of. The low road to orgasm is shorter than the high road. I lived bombarded by porn and surrounded by an ever-changing array of laborers, whom it was easy to imagine staging group assaults for my pleasure. My only real-life sexual encounters happened when I took showers and some Henderson would barge in to check whether I had drowned or warn me that I was using water. Their leering (Doug, pulling the shower curtain back just a hair: "You all right? It's been near ten minutes and I thought you might have fell down and hit your head") taught me to shower like a soldier, cleansing my bits and parts with lightning speed. Sex was clearly potentially the most dangerous and disgusting thing I would ever crave, and I was in no hurry to try it. What I wanted was for Jay to love me. If he had responded to my arm-around-the-shoulder feint by reaching for my underpants, I would have run out of the house.

Maybe I should describe my appearance.

There once lived a famous celebrity who had exactly my face and body, when she was young: Audrey Hepburn.

Before you scoff, imagine a monosyllabic Audrey in an oversize hand-me-down flannel shirt and cuffed jeans with ripped knees. So far, so good. Could even be fashionable, if the shirt opened to reveal her belly button under a chemise. But this Audrey has no waist. Under her tentlike shirt, buttoned to the top, her body appears rectangular. There could be anything in there—a pigeon chest, a potbelly, boils with shunts. While the other girls let their long hair fly free, I tied mine back with rubber bands from the postal service, letting it droop like bunting to hide my face. I needed the rubber bands to see, because I refrained from raising my head. My hands in too-long sleeves clutched the straps of my backpack to reveal flashes of short and grimy fingernail as I clomped my way through school, landing hard on the heels of my translucent plastic sandals, worn in winter with tube socks, hips never shifting to the left or right, my movements seemingly modeled on those of a buffalo. My face, bowed behind its curtain of hair, expressed a quaintly absent-minded dread, a mild inquisitiveness as to what fresh horror might be headed my way, while I routinely blinked back tears.

As a consequence, the resemblance to Audrey was often overlooked.

On two occasions, Jay raided his mother's closet for materiel and posed me in front of her three-way mirror. The first time, it was frightening. He put me in a black lace cocktail dress. I looked like Audrey, but vulnerable and tiny. She never looked weak dressed like that—not to me—but I did. Doubts were sown in my mind about whether she was all that good-looking. After all, she starred in *Funny Face*. A case could be made that she was square-jawed and bat-eared. I made him delete the pictures. The second time made me even sadder. Something like attractiveness shone through the fear, but I mostly saw a fantasy figure suspended over the gulf that separated me from people with disposable income. Jay had put me in at least eight hundred dollars' worth of shoes and clothing. My grandparents in Pasadena never parted from me without slipping me a twenty-dollar bill, which went straight into maintaining my prepaid burner flip phone.

I know now that for certain varieties of straight men—the jealous, the shy, a subset of the devout, etc.—I represented an ideal: a beauty only they know about, a never-cataloged Bellini Madonna that obligingly stores itself in a garbage bag. Jay wanted the opposite. He would have preferred a girl with self-assurance, a prominent Adam's apple, grace, style, a padded ass, five-o'clock shadow.

———

Grandma Tessa could totally see the Audrey thing. She was the first to point it out. My menswear and clomping drove her to distraction. My junior year, she gave me a book by the behavioral hypnotherapist Milton Erickson that was full of case studies of people who had turned their lives around using simple tricks. A gap-toothed woman was too shy and fearful to talk to men, so Erickson commanded her to learn to spit a directed stream of water through the gap. Once she had mastered the skill, he advised her to stake out the water cooler at her office and douse a desirable coworker. One year later, she was married with a baby on the way. Grandma Tessa thought that if I "dressed like a human being," I could be as happy as the woman in the book.

I protested that I lived and worked in a mud pit. More precisely, I lived in a lean-to, with a straight-backed chair in place of a closet, and worked in a mud pit.

She wanted to cut my hair. Hair abatement is a central motif in many of Audrey's films. But I clung to my long hair with intractable loyalty as my one feminine feature, awaiting the day when I would be loved enough to unfurl my secondary sexual characteristics. At that stage they became visible only when I disrobed, as if Torrance were Kabul. She could have shown me how to put my hair up in a bun. She could have realized that twenty dollars every so often was an inadequate allowance for a twenty-first-century teenager. She could have taken me shopping. After graduation, she could have invited me to live in their trailer every other week while I looked for a paid job that didn't involve shoveling horse manure off a flatbed truck and lique-

fying it with a hose. That would have made me prettier overnight! She could have noticed that the Hendersons maintained
an atmosphere of looming sexual menace as a matter of policy.
It was part of how they defined being men: fixation on all things
suggestive, such as breasts in the room, whether in a porn clip,
on a movie star, or in person, attached to an aging alcoholic
friend or a twelve-year-old girl. My underwear in the laundry
upset them. Tampons upset them, even fresh and still in the
box. I kept mine hidden in my backpack and took used ones
straight out to the dumpster, even in the middle of the night.
Grandpa Larry said they smelled up the whole house. Grandma
Tessa could have gotten me the hell out of there when I was ten.

Around college application time, the school counselor asked
me what I wanted to do after graduation.

I said I planned to move to Australia to live with my father.
It sounded more convincing to me than my real plan, which was
to work at the nursery for the foreseeable future. The foreseeable future for me at that time extended for maybe six weeks.
My curiosity about days to come wormed its way forward ten-
tatively and frayed apart, as if I were pushing a rope.

Grandma Tessa and Grandpa Lamont had not gone to college. They had read somewhere that for my generation college
was a bad idea, due to the astronomical cost, so their support
was half-hearted and desultory, as in nonexistent. Grandpa
Lamont said, "You should go to college, honey, if that's what
you want to do. We'll support you in every way we can." I knew
he meant moral support. He had balked at paying for standard-
ized testing.

The Hendersons put no stock in education. Income at Bourdon Farms was measured in leisure hours and followed from clan hierarchy. Having graduated from high school, Axel was kicking back on reduced hours in anticipation of his eventual rise via attrition to top dog after his grandfather and father were dead. Doug split his time between customer acquisition and deliveries—that is, talking on the phone and driving. He had four laborers to draw on (Eric, Roger, me, and sometimes Simon). Grandpa Larry worked on nothing but his bikes.

Maybe my dad in Australia (if he was still there, assuming he ever went) had plenty of money and could have paid for college tuition, my rent in a dorm, and a meal plan at a residence hall, making me independent of the Hendersons. We were not in touch. Obviously it was the modern world, and we could have been video-chatting on holidays and birthdays. But he modeled his behavior on emigrants from the days of sail. I never even got a letter. Do his parents and sister know I exist? Who are they, anyway? His name is Jim Thomas. Try finding a Jim Thomas on the internet!

But my friends were all going to UCLA—that was the plan—and I didn't need college to keep seeing them. It was a straight shot north on the San Diego Freeway, near the VA hospital where Grandpa Larry got his surgeries. Instead of borrowing crazy amounts of money, I would use my graduation money to buy a car.

Maybe it takes a rancid-butter-munching level of negative sophistication to believe UCLA students will maintain social contact with a penniless townie from their high school literary magazine, but I believed it. I believed it with unquestioning faith.

———

My plan didn't work out, because only Jay got into UCLA. Fifi opted to attend Cal Poly. Will chose UCSD. Henry would be off in the fall to Yale, where he had applied without telling Fifi.

Their breakup resounded through the halls of West High and turned our graduation into a hollow formality. Jokey plans to attend proms and parties died on the vine. The only way to keep a social ritual on track was to exclude her, our self-appointed anarchic spirit and voice of reason, or at least a font of more compelling conversational topics than Jay's and Henry's. Will was almost as quiet as I was. Without her, our gatherings malfunctioned. Excluding Henry in her favor was no help. She was angry with all of us, convinced we had known what he was up to all along. School had to end, removing him from her sight, for her to calm down enough to believe us. By then we were all barely talking. Not on account of mutual enmity. We watched a lot of TV that spring. On graduation night, it was at Jay's house with mixed drinks, but it was still TV. Henry drank until he was sick and angry and punched a wall, and Jay nursed him with adhesive bandages and hangover cures from the internet.

Jay's first choice had been UC Irvine, south of Torrance on the way to San Diego. He planned to keep living at home. Not for lack of money to get his own place; his parents' house was simply so big that by age eighteen he was living there almost unnoticed. He had his own fitness room with gigantic mirrors and a parquet floor. He was still taking flamenco lessons from Loretta, still learning rhythms and techniques, and had still not participated in a public recital. Her blindness had progressed until she had almost stopped driving, but she knew there was something odd about his dancing.

The summer before senior year, he had become fatally interested in a dance technique called eurythmy that incorporates spelling. He heard about it from a cousin of Will's who went to a Waldorf school through fourth grade, and learned to imitate it off the internet.

In eurythmy, a dancer's movements encode letters of the alphabet. Thus texts can be danced in a way that is not abstract or imagistic but digital. He started writing flash micro-poems and incorporating them into his flamenco routines.

I did not attend his college auditions or even hear about them, but UC Irvine did not award him a scholarship for its BFA program in dance, nor did Cal State Long Beach. Both schools rejected him outright, like a sex offender. So I have no trouble imagining the squirming jury as Loretta's arthritic *répétiteur* flailed out a *bulerías* with a thick brown thumbnail and Jay twirled, stomping erratically, elbows high, to spell "S-E-M-E-N-S-H-I-N-E."

He was admitted to UCLA's school of humanities and the arts on the strength of the usual transcript and essay or—conceivably—parental intervention. Dancing was permitted there, in conjunction with research in critical dance studies, but not encouraged.

Nonetheless he felt that his Art had gotten him in the door, because it was so super gay. "Colleges crave diverse student bodies like mine," he said—as though the art school rejections had never happened. Jay had faith in himself. He learned from experience what he wanted to learn and forgot the rest.

———

As promised, Grandma Tessa and Grandpa Lamont gave me five hundred dollars in cash in exchange for my diploma, which they framed and hung on the wall of their living room.

The money was enough to buy a subtly rhomboid Mazda (it had been in an accident that skewed the chassis) and kit it out with retreads and stolen Nevada plates. Doug took me to Barstow on the back of his motorbike to pick it up.

I did not know how to drive. Grandpa Larry had learned the hard way, via Doug and Axel, that a child who can drive will borrow a truck and raise hell in it, while an unlicensed "illegal alien" drives only on command and as gingerly as if he were hauling eggshells in a vehicle made of eggshells. So he let the laborers drive, but not me.

I taught myself by driving around the desert for four days, sleeping on the back bench seat at night, until I felt capable of bringing the car home.

My progress back toward Los Angeles was slow. The muffler was rusted through, and at higher speeds it sounded like an airplane. When I got home, Axel taped up the muffler as his present.

I drove with fake inspection stickers and no insurance, title, or license. The police in California never stopped me. Thin white privilege, I guess.

But to enjoy any privilege whatsoever seemed fair enough to me when I started, and to risk my liberty and solvency by persisting seemed fair enough later on. The real privilege would have been to live without dithering, in a better universe.

———

In communicating with me, the Hendersons often employed a cruel sincerity they believed was sarcasm, which in turn they believed to be a humorous variety of lighthearted irony, which is why at first I thought it was a joke when they told me that as a full-time worker at Bourdon Farms I would need to pay rent. The bill had started coming due the day I turned seventeen (they pinned adulthood to eligibility to join the army), but they had agreed to defer collection until I graduated.

To be fair, they offered me better conditions than they did Roger and Eric, who shared a room. "Or you can pick up evening shifts somewhere and pay us in cash," Doug offered. "Five hundred a month would do it. It doesn't matter to us! But you have to pull your weight." He assured me that I was a key asset to the operation, which needed my help with a big order of topiary. I asked him for a loan to buy a computer. He gave me fifty dollars—a bonus graduation gift, he said, in memory of my mother.

I invested in a used, bootleg Mexican Windows smartphone without its own SIM card. For the sake of privacy (I suspected Axel of sniffing router traffic), I went out to a coffee shop with wifi to look for another place to live.

There were rooms I could afford that wanted me. A woman in her eighties, her house full of card tables piled high with magazines she had been sorting for decades, offered me a cot in her garage. A couple was willing to trade their spare bedroom for fifty hours of childcare a week so the wife could get a job. A retired naval officer showed me a derelict truck camper in his side yard. His eyes were bloodshot. He trembled as he petted his dogs.

I filled out job applications at gas stations, restaurants, cafés, and convenience stores. But all my work experience had been gained performing unskilled labor or reading stories and poetry. I had never handled money. I had never operated a dishwasher. I falsified nothing but my Social Security number, unaware that job applicants are expected, encouraged—even required, should they have felony convictions—to lie.

The topiary order was eight hundred bushes, each a cone topped with a sphere. The consensus at Bourdon Farms was that no man could compete with my talent for shaping privet, and that it would have been a crime against the customer to let anyone else do the work.

I could hold the gas-powered hedge clippers up at shoulder level for the space of about two bushes, but there were eight hundred. I ended up working on a high ladder, cutting spheres five feet from the ground with my back humped like a ferret's. In the afternoons, I swayed. My coworkers occasionally swung by to call out, "You okay?"

I pleaded with Doug and Axel, volunteering to teach Eric and Roger so they could help me. The topiaries kept growing, and by myself I was so slow that by the time I had finished a hundred or so, I had to go back and touch them up. They both looked at me funny. "Of course they know how to cut topiary," Doug said. "That's not the point. The question is, how well do they cut topiary. How conscientiously. You're the absolute best." Axel nodded in agreement with his father. "Shaping it over and over is the idea," Doug added. "That gives it time to fill out. That's what gives Bourdon Farms products the quality that commands a premium price."

They said they could seal a deal for my back rent, swap it for work, even raise my (cashless) wage. I tried not to look grateful when Doug made the offer, puffed up with magnanimity like a pigeon.

Jay opted for UCLA's on-campus housing, leasing half of a two-bedroom suite. I understood his motivation. The college was only twenty miles away and he could drive there in half an hour, assuming it was three a.m. on a Tuesday. At nearly any other time, the drive took twice as long. Its dorm communities made up a city within a city, exclusively populated by bright and vetted youth. Thousands of available single men milled around picturesque lawns between skyscraper-like dorms, mingling in food-court-like restaurants. The residences were segregated by family resources, but the dining halls allowed rich and poor students to intermix.

Within the first week, he had taken part in a postmodern dance workshop and befriended a poet named Rick, a grad student in his thirties who still ate in the food courts—no longer enrolled, but working on his doctoral dissertation in the library. His thesis in the history of medicine on eighteenth-century pseudoparasites was not progressing, he told Jay, because of his passion for the epic poem. He was working on one about François-Dominique Toussaint L'Ouverture. It was already ten thousand lines long, more than eight hundred stanzas, each line backed up by meticulous research.

"Wow," I said when Jay told me. He said that his response had been similar, but that Rick was an interesting dude and that the history of medicine was freaky.

For weeks, Jay drifted from building to building around the campus, peeking into lectures and talking to passersby. Dance studies alone would not produce enough credits to graduate, so he tried out economics, history, gender studies, Slavic studies, food studies, and the English department. There, in a freshman seminar, a boy caught his eye.

I went to see him via public transit on the third Friday in October, packing my sleeping bag. I took a lot of flak from the Hendersons for cutting out on the weekend only three months before their topiaries were due for transplant.

That Jay had met someone was something I deduced from his behavior, not from anything he said. He bought me my meals, all of which I found delicious. While we were eating, he kept casting his eyes around. He never saw the person he wanted to show me. He never mentioned him once. But I knew he was out there.

In the morning, he drove us up into the hills behind Westwood in his SUV, talking about his classes. Slavic studies had turned out to be rich in intriguing material, such as disparaging medieval Islamic descriptions of the Vikings' treatment of women. Even English literature had proven tawdry and risqué.

The tidbits he told me on our walk were obscene, but they were scholarship, not porn: information for its own sake, not to serve a purpose. They made me feel a weird sort of indefinable arousal, a magnetic absence that was not sexual, drawing me toward books as if snobby dark-age Arabs and louche metaphysical poets might be my new best friends.

In the evening we walked around the business district and then up and down fraternity row, looking at bars and parties without going inside. After a while we talked about what we saw, because his inventory of disjointed tidbits was used up.

On Sunday, he showed me the university campus, including the art museum (there was a costume exhibition) and the library and various imposing trees and architectural ensembles. Then I rode home.

For people in Jay's family, getting a degree was basic hygiene, like washing behind your ears. He took no steps to convince me that it was fulfilling or worthwhile. He said it was hard work, but with good food—looking around as he said this, keeping constant watch for someone in particular. He was blasé and on edge. I could tell he was nursing an incommunicable new feeling like mine.

CHAPTER THREE

We did not see each other for several weeks, and then it was almost Thanksgiving. Henry's parents had waited until he went off to Yale to get a non-amicable divorce. They were fighting in court about the RV dealership and even the dog, which was fourteen and had an autoimmune skin disease. The dog should have been put down, but they preferred to fight about it. It was clear that instead of coming home, Henry would get himself invited to someone's house on the East Coast.

Will was coming home and looked forward to seeing us all. He said San Diego was a stuffy town full of retired naval officers, but the beaches kicked ass.

Fifi did not like San Luis Obispo. The beauty she had cherished as a visitor struck her, after she moved there, as mere vegetation and rocks, and the students were unadventurous. She wanted to transfer to UCSD, because she missed Will the most of all her friends (a transparent lie), or Berkeley if she could get in.

I got all this information secondhand, from Jay, via oral flip-phone conversation. My new smartphone had heated up suddenly and died of fever, leaving me without internet access. I could no longer use the PCs in our school library, and I could not prove my residency to get a public library card. Not having a computer was a major factor in my belief that I would never work anywhere but the nursery.

The information rundown had sounded comprehensive, so I was surprised when Jay turned up at Thanksgiving with a new friend.

They picked me up in Fifi's car. I was late getting out to 190th—Fifi claimed she wanted to avoid the potholes in our driveway—and the car stood in a parking bay on the other side of the street.

"This is Peter!" Jay called out joyfully from the open window. "Peter, meet Bran! Look where she lives!" He gesticulated at the gate of Bourdon Farms. He scooched over to sit touching the new boy (it was a very small car), and I got in.

Once we were moving, Fifi bounced in her seat, put the car in neutral, and said, "Bet I can make it to the PCH without turning on the ignition."

I noticed that she looked different. Her chenille top was paired with skinny jeans—she was smaller—and her hair was up.

"Don't do that," Will said. "Your car has power steering."

"Peter's never been to the beach!" Jay said jubilantly. "He's from Maine!"

"Maine has beaches," Will said. "There's Cape Cod."

"Cape Cod is in the People's Republic of Massachusetts," Fifi said. She seemed to be unconsciously needling the absent Henry, another staunch Democrat.

"You've never seen a beach?" I asked Peter.

He ignored my question and said, "I love your name. Is it short for Branwen?"

"Brandy," I said.

I gripped the back of Will's seat as he said, "Fifi! Stop sign!" She had done a classic California stop at the blinking red light halfway down the hill, riding the brake as she ran right through it. She giggled, and I realized she was high. "Turn on the car!" he protested. "The steering wheel can lock up!"

"There's no need," she said. "You're just jealous because you can't drive stick." She continued down the hill in neutral.

"That has nothing to do with anything," he insisted, earnestly.

She started the car when we ran out of momentum going up the next hill, but on our way down the final big hill to the PCH she shut it off again and raised both hands as if we were on a roller coaster.

"I love this road," Peter said obligingly. "It's like the groundswell."

"Jesus, Fifi!" Will said. She had seen the red light at the PCH and applied her feet to the clutch and the brake, but very much at her own pace. A diesel horn blasted in our ears. A tall pickup truck roared by our front bumper. We came to a stop blocking the highway's right lane.

No one said another word. The light changed in our favor, and she started the car and put it in reverse. A right turn would have made more sense, but she preferred to start over.

When the honking was done and we were back at the light, I said, "Can I drive?"

Jay pointed out that I didn't have a license and that they were all high, because Will had found access to super-potent weed at UCSD.

"I'll drive," Peter volunteered, opening his door quickly. Fifi was slower, but by the time the light cycled, they had traded places. "Where are we going?"

"Venice," Jay said. "There's this poetry reading at an art center in Venice. Just stay on the PCH."

"Who do you know here?" I asked Peter.

"I go to college with Jay. We're friends."

I looked at Jay, seated next to me, eyes front, smiling and staring at the side of Peter's face. Wondering why, I followed his gaze.

Peter's cheeks were pale as milk, with a bluish cast where he shaved. His eyes were black. In the rearview mirror it was impossible to tell where the irises ended and the pupils began. His large, square hands rested gently on the wheel. A mass of black curly hair bounced with every jolt of the overloaded Honda. Reddish highlights, like the points on a bay horse, reflected the setting sun each time we passed an east-west street. He was chiaroscuro, almost two-toned, like the most coveted cats and cows. Pale clothes (white Oxford cloth, chinos), black sneakers.

The people outside the art center, an old motel whose rooms had been turned into artists' studios, had never heard of the poetry reading. The lobby was locked and dark. We pooled dollar bills to park at the beach so we could show Peter the ocean. Will took off his shoes and waded into the surf. Jay frolicked, running in circles on the sand and carrying Fifi piggyback.

Peter asked me what I knew about Branwen. "The Welsh Cinderella," he promptly explained. "She marries an Irish king who puts her to work in the kitchen, and trains a starling to talk so it can take an SOS to her brother in Wales. It ends badly."

"I don't know about Welsh stuff," I said. "I used to like Arthurian legend."

"Nice," he said. "I want to do part of my honors thesis on the Matter of Britain. The aesthetics of magical weapons. Not the effects, but the texts that power them. You know Arnold Schön-berg, the originator of twelve-tone music, the composer—he designed a kabbalistic doomsday weapon that was a sequence of musical tones [. . .]."

(Throughout this text, I will employ the token "[. . .]" to indicate inability to quote, paraphrase, or reconstruct things Peter said.)

My mind phased into a spaced-out condition while my eyes vainly sought a focal point in the empty middle distance. Absently I gazed upon the western horizon. Scattered golden stars perforated the deep blue of oncoming night. Venus looked directly back at me, making eye contact through her pinprick in the sky, sending a crystal-clear message: Hold fast to this dude. Do not let him get away!

Willets were calling on the beach, saying the same thing. But how? Peter finished talking, and I said, "Most of the books I have are about Arthurian legend."

He nodded sympathetically in grave understanding, look-ing scholarly, and said, "It is such a relief to meet someone who can hear the word 'magic' without wanting to talk about J. K. Rowling."

There, I had something apropos to say. "She made Merlin a student at her *boarding school*!" I said, in the bitter tones of a resentful child discovering too late that it has been tricked. "*Merlin* learned everything he knows at *Hogwarts*. What a—what a—" I struggled to find a word that meant "commer-cialistic parvenu who thinks she can hijack the cachet of my favorite ancient myth by dumping on it." I failed, but in Peter's presence I believed there might be a word.

He said, "Rowling is irrelevant to discussions of magic. Those books are about social segregation and dominance."

"House elves!" I said. Even I could tell they were enslaved. Born to serve, they never made any money.

"Subhuman," he said. "And the Muggles are Slavs, but she mercifully stays her hand. It's all very British. A Continental fascist would have had them digging their own graves in something other than metaphorical terms."

Back at the art center, the lobby's lights were on and its denizens looked like poets, so we waited outside on benches. Around ten o'clock a bearded man showed up with PA equipment and revealed that the reading was supposed to start around eleven. We were all drooping and hungry by then, so we gave up, and Peter drove us to a coffee shop, where he talked Japanese popular culture with Fifi. She suddenly seemed to know a lot about it.

The next day, I got an early call from Jay. Peter wanted to see Compton and the Watts Towers, for reasons related to art history and hip-hop. Jay, Fifi, and Will all nominally owned cars, but those cars were registered to their parents, who refused to let them be carjacked in "the hood." To please Peter and keep him a happy tourist, Jay needed my car.

People farther north call Torrance the hood. Jay sited the hood to the northeast, toward Culver City, while Henry had once remarked in my presence that Hollywood was the hood. Compton might as well have been the blank space on an old seafaring chart, with krakens and maelstroms.

I, for my part, had been to neither Compton nor Watts. They were off limits, devoid of Bourdon Farms clients, rich in the people Grandpa Larry called "spicks" and "spades." I hoped for vicious traffic, so that the trip would take an extra long time.

I would spend it next to Peter, who would sit up front to get a better view, assuming Jay did not insist on being up front to navigate.

To my joy, Jay insisted that Peter had longer legs. He folded himself into the rear seat and followed our route on an app.

He was wrong. He was tall and gangly, and Peter was only medium-tall. But it was easier for Jay, a dancer, to sit with his knees up under his chin.

I found out how they had gotten to be friends. Peter was helping Jay get up to speed academically. The seminar where they had met was somehow an introduction to critical theory. I had no idea what critical theory was supposed to be, and neither did Jay, even after two months of class. Having enjoyed his ebullient efforts at participation, Peter had begun tutoring him for fun, as a distraction, because he already knew everything people learn freshman year, or maybe in all of college.

"I was doing okay without you—admit it," Jay said.

"'Okay' is a trap," Peter said. "Adjuncts reward you for it, because it's easiest for them if everybody has the same response and you all write identical papers. If you let them have their way, they will guarantee that no one in a position to advance your career ever takes you seriously."

"It probably matters more if you want a career," Jay said.

"You signed up for four years," Peter said. "You should be getting more for your money than a crash course in plagiarism."

"I only care about dance. I'm majoring in English just to keep my freedom, so nobody tries to tell me how to dance."

"Have you seen him dance?" I asked Peter. Jay made a dissatisfied noise, but I said anyway, "His teacher is blind."

Peter looked over and made eye contact, as though delighted by this information more than he could say. "Sweet," he said.

"I'm reliving Kafka's response to the news that Gustav Janouch got a job playing piano at the 'cinema of the blind.'" Getting no reaction, he went on, "He was a student who published a book of his conversations with Kafka. In Prague, in central Europe. The writer Kafka. Gustav Janouch played piano to make money when he was a teenager. In a movie theater where the proceeds benefited the blind, like a Disabled American Veterans Thrift Store. Not for blind people."

I knew that Kafka was a deep and mysterious writer, his work somehow related to the very finest science fiction, but I had nothing to say. I felt bad for making fun of Jay.

"Dancers should all be blind," Peter went on. "Composers should be deaf, and writers should be illiterate. I like your Mazda, by the way. It's only fair I be reminded of British Mithraism and [. . .] when I'm on my way to Compton. Have you been there before?"

"You're a good dancer," I said to Jay. "Sorry."

"Never ever!" Jay said to Peter, ignoring me. "You're the first reason I ever had to go there."

We cruised around Compton until we found a non-chain diner with all-day breakfast. It had no parking lot, so I had to explore a little to find parking on a residential street.

Walking to the diner, I hung back behind them on the narrow sidewalk. Peter walked with slow circumspection, as if he were middle-aged. But his gestures were quick and his mind skipped away to distant associations while Jay's stood fluttering like a banner on a flagpole. Jay was a kite and Peter was a stunt jet, mentally. Physically, it was the other way around. Peter's body was tense but steady. And I was an empty cargo plane in a holding pattern, waiting for signals from the tower.

The diner felt nostalgic inside, as if we were revisiting a

past we had not been alive for. The tables were topped with abalone-patterned red melamine and rimmed with a dully shining metal like nickel or magnesium. The bacon was cold and there was chocolate in the bread pudding. Peter talked to the waitress for at least five minutes. She was a recent arrival from Texas, middle-aged and blond. The other patrons looked Chicano. I suddenly remembered that he had wanted to see Black culture, and the inanity, the near-asininity of his wanting to experience a sketchy part of town because of a record album from the eighties (*Straight Outta Compton,* featuring "Fuck tha Police") cast a pall of confusion over me. I was embarrassed that he wanted to see Black people, and embarrassed not to have found him any. I did not want either of us to be that ridiculous.

I asked him whether Compton was what he expected.

"I wasn't looking for anything specific," he said. "Definitely not gang warfare with blood in the streets. To see that, you'd probably need three months and a camouflage blind, like a filmmaker trying to see jaguars mating. That's why they have TV. It's the place, Compton, that's significant to me, not the reality. I wanted the sensation of eating all-day-breakfast in a sacred site."

"Like having lunch in Avalon," I said. "The town on Catalina Island. You go there from Long Beach or San Pedro. I wanted to see King Arthur when I was nine, so my mom took us there on the boat."

"Did you see him?"

"I know he doesn't exist. I still wanted to see him. I know he lives under Glastonbury Tor."

"I wouldn't mind having lunch in Avalon. I've never been to a mythical paradise."

"The boat to Avalon is like eighty bucks," I said, with unwitting pathos. "It's a once-in-a-lifetime thing."

"L.A. is one big mythical paradise," Jay said. "Come on, let's flake on Watts and go to Griffith Park. You know the place I'm talking about? Where James Dean has the knife fight in *Rebel Without a Cause*?"

"My car won't make it up the hill with three people." This time the pathos was deliberate, and Jay laughed.

"You can take me there one night," Peter said to me.

I made eye contact, because I was so surprised. "If I have time," I said. "I work a lot."

"We can take my car," Jay said. "It has three hundred horsepower."

I throttled—in the sense of strangled—my disappointment and said brightly, "Good idea!"

Over our BLTs, I asked Peter whether he had been to L.A. before he arrived for college.

"No," he said. "I was supposed to go to Harvard up to the last minute, and I bailed. Like I was walking into a roach motel and I'd never get unglued. Coming here was an act of rebellion. When you're from the East Coast, where everything is old, this whole state feels painted on, like it was thrown together yesterday. Like a film set, a thin layer of asphalt over sand, bordered with plastic palm trees. It's how I imagine postmodernity, improvised and dynamic and vulgar. Places like Cambridge are about hanging on to your own. Ancient rights of property. It has like dining halls from the eighteen hundreds, and petty nobility descended from colonial officials. It's decadent."

"But L.A. is even more ancient," Jay said. "We have Spanish missions and Indian tribes. That's why it has a Spanish name."

"Sure, but how many people have actually been here longer than twenty years?"

"Most of my family came here in the sixties, and Bran's people are like hillbillies from the eighteen hundreds."

"It's my common-law stepfamily," I said. "But yeah, they think they're the real natives, and the Indians are fake and white and in it for the gaming." Peter smiled, so I continued. "My common-law stepfather—not my real stepfather, but like a stepfather—told me once the real Indians are the Anasazi, where there's nothing left but their cliff dwellings, and the Navajo who live there now are like, 'Don't look at us!'"

Jay said, "Like what Peter told me about how the real Europeans are extinct and everybody who lives there now is from like Kyrgyzstan."

"Close," he said. "I was saying how few genetic traces we have from Celtic and Roman Britain in today's DNA. The Visigoths were very thorough. And no one knows who the Aurignacians who decorated Altamira and Lascaux even were, or whether they were modern humans or Neanderthals or what. Not that I'd call any Europeans interlopers."

I told them about how I sometimes thought my grandfather and his pals might have chased off the original owners of Bourdon Farms, because of certain telling gaps in his collection of creaky photo albums. "He's like, 'Look, here's Grandpa with our old truck,' but he never shows you a picture of his mother, or his wife, or himself when he was little. Those photo albums could have come with the house."

"Wouldn't it be easy to check?" Peter said. "Even if everything looks like a film set here, there are public records of land ownership."

"I looked it up. It's owned by the state."

The waitress turned up her TV to drown us out and refilled our coffee for free, and Peter said, "God, I love this place." Looking around at the yellowing houseplants and crooked curtains, he added, "I feel so at home in this—this basin?—L.A. County? I'm so glad I skipped Harvard." He put his hand on the table, grazing my pinkie finger with his. "This shallow world makes thinking seem deeper. All the history seeping out of archives on the East Coast clogs up your mind like cement. There are no arrogant artifacts out here, waiting to shout you down."

I wanted to tell him about the La Brea Tar Pits, but Jay had gone from smiling beatifically to looking worried. He asked Peter, "Do you think I'm shallow?"

"You and Bran are the deepest things for miles around," Peter told him. "There's nothing interesting here to distract me from you, believe me." He put his hand squarely on my hand and squeezed.

I was used to things being weird, but not to their being pleasant at the same time. I could feel that I was being fucked with, and I liked it a lot.

Watts was delightful. The towers were beautiful, delicate, and impressive. Then it was time for me to drive the two of them home for Thanksgiving dinner.

Jay's father invited me in, saying it was at the behest of Jay's mother, who was out back and would love to see me. But I was committed to warm up TV dinners for the Hendersons. Sometimes I spent holidays with Grandma Tessa and Grandpa Lamont, but they were in Tampa visiting their son, Uncle Jerry.

He had become estranged from my mother when she hooked up with Doug, and dropped her completely when she abandoned me. I barely remembered him.

Thanksgiving at Bourdon Farms was always a downer. The only fun holiday was the Fourth of July, when the bikers held a barbecue and dirt bike race that Grandpa Larry said had originally been run with mustangs. But he also claimed that his great-grandfather had spent every Christmas at a convent fucking novices, and every New Year's at a camp in the desert hunting death-row inmates with an exclusive club consisting of the state's most respected politicians and judges and their dogs. The real world did not play much of a role in Grandpa Larry's inner life, except as a source of cash.

I, too, however, am guilty of playing down reality as I tell this story, sticking to elements that bear directly on its wish-fulfillment endgame, as if I had not been spending forty-plus hours a week laundering the Hendersons' money with a dusty bandanna around my sweaty head, in my work sneakers that smelled like cheese.

My omissions follow the same narrative principle as Grandpa Larry's or Tolkien's. Tolkien worked the trenches of the Somme before drafting a new mythology that culminated in *The Return of the King*, and Grandpa Larry likewise invested the drab routine of a small-time gangster (I think his ill-gotten gains came from holding contraband until people picked it up) with the glory of flamboyant sin. My work was performed in a moonscape of busted equipment and untrustworthy men, safer than the Somme, but similarly pointless. The plants lived and died in long rows, blissfully insensate cannon fodder in the never-ending war between supply and demand.

So why talk about it? My work was the only survival strategy that I—an ignorant child—happened to know. That hardly makes it interesting.

When I met unfulfilled middle-class people later on (meaning neither teachers, rich wheeler-dealers, pediatricians, nor public defenders, but workers with do-nothing, bullshit office jobs), it became clear to me that white-collar proletarians get off easy. They know all about watching the clock, but not about mixing ennui with the kind of pain that bodes ill for life past thirty.

Sensible people avoid hard work at any cost. My mother left. The Hendersons retire young. The laborers never stay long. I was the one person tied to Bourdon Farms by class. The ignorant child who knew no other life, the perfect employee, taught to accept self-harm as an economic necessity.

Anyway, we got together the next day at Will's house. He and Jay played a pseudo-fantasy video game while Fifi, Peter, and I pretended to watch them, at least for a while. I had tried the game years before and died over and over while losing. Peter praised various psychedelic Japanese games we had never seen that were full of surreal imagery and flowing bright colors. Fifi claimed not to need cannabis to appreciate games like that, because she was in touch with her inner child.

Peter said, "I don't think I have one."

"Everybody does," she said, shifting her weight and adjusting her miniskirt. "You outgrow it, and then there it is."

"I mean, I think I never had to internalize it. My emotional existence has a strong continuity to it. It feels linear. I've had the same personality for as long as I can remember."

"Then you have an outer child," she said.

I found that plausible, given his extroverted ways and smooth skin, and said, "Spot on!"

Peter looked at me and said, "I wouldn't criticize in your position, with your inarticulacy, and your oversize clothes, and your unkempt hair, and your mismatched socks."

His tone was kind, not insulting, and not knowing what to say, I said nothing. I was thinking that those things were characteristic of all the adults I saw regularly, the exceptions being teachers and Will's parents. I could not honestly apply the description to myself, since I was not those things. My identity was whatever I was naked, and not some cyborg conglomeration of skills and socks.

"Bran is not now and has never been a child," Fifi asserted.

"What were you?" Peter asked. "A child soldier?"

"I don't know," I said. "I grew up fast. Kids are helpless suckers. I've been looking for a clean break since I was five." I was trying to sound naked, and my voice got a bit thin and whiny.

Nobody said anything at first. "You must know how pitiful that sounds," Peter ventured.

"I don't mean anybody abused me," I said. "I don't know what I meant."

"The term 'helpless sucker' denotes a trusting, dependent person, right? But it's reasonable to be trusting and dependent when you're five."

I looked away, sniveling, and said, "Five is pretty old to be trusting and dependent."

"I was a happy kid. My parents were gentle and nice. That's what I meant, when I said I had nothing to repress. But even an adult needs more from life than simple freedom from abuse and violence."

Fifi said, "Your inner child is showing! Look, everybody— Bran's crying!"

Jay dropped the game controls and turned to hug me. He smothered me a bit, but only because I dropped my head almost to his navel.

"I'm sorry," Peter said, touching my sleeve. I backed away from Jay and smiled up at him.

"Bran's volatile," Fifi declared. "Like a shy woodland creature."

"What's your family life like?" Peter asked me.

Fifi said firmly, "She does not *have* a family. She's an orphan held captive by slavers. She's not even related to them! She's just got nowhere else to go."

Peter put his arm around my shoulders to give me a squeeze and said, "You really are Branwen. No, it's worse than that, because you're not a queen but an outlaw. *Homo sacer,* condemned to bare life under the disciplinary state of exception [...]."

We were all thinking, Homosexual soccer? Is that new internet slang? But the reference was to the Latin title of a book by Giorgio Agamben, an Italian disciple of Foucault, and it meant I was fair game. Open season on me.

ay sent me Peter's phone number and email address, with an attached message from Peter saying that I should get in touch if I was ever near UCLA.

I waited about a week before texting Peter that I had to deliver poinsettias to a church in Westwood on a Saturday morning—a falsehood—and that we could have breakfast when I was done.

He suggested a chain doughnut shop outside the VA hospital. I think he was being considerate, because he knew it was near big parking lots and he thought I might be driving a truck. I had been there with Doug once, when Grandpa Larry was getting a skin graft for the malignant melanoma on his forehead. I remembered enormous posters depicting shiny doughnuts—they looked wet—and laminated orange tables. An understandably surly worker had poured coffee so hot I could barely touch the doubled paper cup. I imagined sitting there with Peter for hours, waiting for our coffee to cool.

When I arrived, he was drinking apple juice and reading a book. He put it in his messenger bag and said, "I'd pull out a chair for you, but . . ." The seating was attached to the tables, each chair composed of two squares of molded plastic loosely held to metal struts with screws.

I apologized—apologizing was insane and I knew it, but my

knowing made it okay, it seemed to me—and fetched myself a coffee. He asked how my errand had gone.

I said, "I didn't have anything to do in Westwood. I drove here to see you."

He said, "That's nice to hear. I wasn't sure what to say to you. I don't usually have breakfast at this hour, but it's my fault for telling you to get in touch when you were around, instead of just inviting you to dinner."

"It's fine. I like doughnuts. Do you live near here?"

"Pretty close," he said. "It's like a mile. It's a nice walk. Do you want to go there? It's more comfortable. I have armchairs."

"Good idea," I said. "I can't drink this coffee here anyway. It's too hot."

I am still impressed by the strange efficiency with which we sought privacy. Why did I trust him—because my arteries were flooded with oxytocin? I stood up and got myself a lid.

We left the Mazda in the lot and hiked up the hill to campus. While we walked, he asked about my common-law step-family and why on earth I called them that, given that there was no common-law marriage in California. I explained that it was Doug's concept, because he wanted the world to know that he had been a good husband to my mother, even though he never divorced his first wife. I shared some classic tales of Grandpa Larry. He wanted to know whether Axel was nice. I claimed that no one knew anything about Axel's personality, because he continually readapted to fit in with the other Hendersons, and that they all did that, basing their notion of what it takes to be a Henderson on an outdated ideal of masculinity handed down not from cowboy ancestors but from the Terminator movies.

"Do they have girlfriends?" he asked. "You never mention anyone female."

"They have all kinds of girlfriends."

"But no relationships."

"No."

"Now you remind me of the legend of Deirdre," he said. "Not literally. She's a beautiful woman in a Scottish legend who lived with three brothers. I know you're not involved with the Hendersons, but maybe they're involved with you. Do you have any idea how pretty you are?"

"No."

I was hoping he would tell me, but instead he said, "You need to get out of there. Just drop it and go. Did you ever read Kafka's *The Castle*? It's a novel about feeling responsible for things that aren't your responsibility. This guy hears that he's wanted for some reason by the lord of some castle, so he goes there and tries to get an appointment and find out why, and ends up spending his whole life hanging around this nowhere village, waiting. You're kind of the same, waiting instead of escaping, because you think you're implicated in these guys' lives. But, I mean, they're not related to you, and it doesn't sound like they even like you. When push comes to shove, what do you even have to do with them?"

"It's my home," I said. "They give me work and food and a place to stay. I don't have any money."

"You finished high school, right?"

"I had to," I said. "My grandma promised me five hundred dollars if I graduated."

He was silent. Then he said, "You do know how pitiful that sounds, right? Do you?"

"Do I what?"

He was silent again and said, "You're making me want to intervene."

Around that time, we reached his dorm. He was occupied in saying hello to other students as we climbed the stairs. I said nothing and watched my step, hiding behind my hair.

He had the cheapest kind of single room available, in a cramped suite with four other students. They had all gone home for the weekend. His room was small and narrow, like a nun's cell. It had a window at the end, a desk under a high bunk bed, and storage cabinets on both sides next to the door. Airless and stuffy, it was heaped on every side with stacks of books. Not large or colorful ones like the trade paperback classic novels and coffee-table books about tourist destinations in our school library, but tiny books that traveled in herds, sets by the same authors in identical bindings. From what I could see and imagine, they included the most revelatory philosophical works known to history, the most spellbinding tomes of arcane wisdom ever rediscovered, and the greatest stories ever told, from the ancient Sumerians to the latest algorithms, all gathered into a curated canon like the library of Alexandria, and he knew them all by heart.

He kept pulling down books. Plutarch, according to him, had described Cleopatra as someone who was not exceptionally good-looking, but so educated and clever that great men followed her around like ducklings. Also, Anne Frank was a teenager famous for keeping a diary while hiding from the law, a.k.a. the Nazis, who were the law in Nazi-occupied Europe, which just goes to show you that lawbreaking can be justified, as argued by Henry David Thoreau, but not in *Walden,* which is about how people with money lead lives of quiet desperation. He explained what he meant by joking that I had been kidnapped by Spartans. He summarized the plots of *A Room of One's Own, Paradise Lost, One-Dimensional Man,* and *Com-*

ing of Age in Mississippi. To illustrate the magical powers of text, he recited Satanist black-metal lyrics, read me a poem by Paul Celan—his best-known one, a series of incantatory repetitions cobbled together from other poets' scraps—and lent me a tattered book with his name in cursive inside the front cover, *The Gentle Art of Verbal Self-Defense.*

Then it was lunchtime. I had overstayed our breakfast date by a lot, so I left.

Back at Bourdon Farms, I took my new book way out into a stand of aspens rooted in plastic sacks and sat down to read it on a pile of shipping pallets. At first it upset me. I realized that I did have an outer child. Instead of taking steps to preserve my mental integrity, I had let the Hendersons corner me. I had lain there squeaking like a blind kitten, waiting for help from some random onlooker. The random onlooker had finally arrived in the form of Peter, but his lending of the book made it clear that I was expected to save myself. I was not ready. Any attempt on my part to include verbal self-defense and the Hendersons in the same sentence made me panicky.

Then I remembered what he had said about Kafka's castle. It was what I had been saying to myself all along. There was no need for defenses! I could walk away from Bourdon Farms, as soon as I found someplace to go.

Without telling Jay, I visited Peter again twice in his room in December before he left for Christmas in Maine. He said that my mind had been lamed by long years of passive acceptance of my living conditions, and that it would become more agile if I accepted that humanity was collectively tragic. To undergird his case, he told me about colonialism and the Holocaust. Generally speaking, he felt I should know all about them. Colonialism was a major disaster, with missionaries systematically destroying cultures and doing irreparable damage to ecosystems and subjugating and killing entire populations. Even the Holocaust, which I had assumed had been blown way out of proportion, was way, way worse than the Hendersons liked to make out. They claimed that the Jews worked too many hours on too little food in Auschwitz and died of starvation like the Russians under Stalin and the Chinese under Mao, the idea being to let me draw flattering comparisons between Auschwitz, the Gulags, and the Great Leap Forward and the abundance I enjoyed at Bourdon Farms. Peter said the Jews of Europe had been murdered by the millions for no reason, many while still plump and healthy.

His logic was that familiarity with the Belgian Congo and Treblinka would cure me of thinking tragedy had anything to do with individual fate, which in turn would cure me of thinking my problems were my fault. Primo Levi and friends would teach me that perpetrators of crimes against humanity lost their right to be tragic. Their humanity was gone, sacrificed on the altar of a mechanistic fantasy. What was humanity? It was a dignified state of resigned, intelligent, stoical courage that came from valuing human life. What was human life? It was not survival but freedom and self-actualization.

I asked my grandparents whether I could move in with them, in violation of their lease. Grandpa Lamont said, "Your commute would be terrible!"

After he got over the shock of being afraid Grandma Tessa

would say yes, the two of them explained that I was all grown up and responsible for myself. They claimed to have thought of inviting me earlier—the trailer park management might have made an exception—but I was such a shy child that they feared I would not survive separation from my friend Jay.

I chose not to fight with them about the past. But there would never have been a reason to stop seeing Jay. Through him, I would still have met the others. There was nobody in Pasadena to make me pull all-nighters cutting topiary by flood-light for no wages. I could have had extracurricular activities, more friends, or an after-school job that paid. I could have gotten good grades and a scholarship to college. And they could have lost their home. Debates about the past solved nothing.

Over Christmas, I spent my spare time with Jay, who talked constantly about Peter. I had often heard him pine for waiters and fitness instructors he barely spoke to. This time was differ-ent. All semester, he had averaged at least an hour a day talking with Peter over meals and coffees. He knew him way too well to think he was gay. But he also knew nothing about his taste in partners. Were there any women he liked?

The topic fascinated me as well, but neither of us could offer robust data. In conversation, Peter reveled in description, categorizing all facets of everything with surgical ruthlessness. Simple categories such as "hot or not" did not map onto his exhaustive array of sometimes brutal criteria.

I demanded to know how Peter described me. "Butch," Jay said immediately. "Hmm. Slouches so you can't see her face. Dresses like a lumberjack. Charming face, but when she looks up, you expect a mustache. Umm, what else. Cylindrical limbs, like a ballet dancer. Walks like a muscle-bound sylph . . . I know! He said you're dirty."

"*Butch?*" I said.

"Bran," he said indulgently. He reached over and shook the sleeve of my flannel shirt as if he expected it to rattle.

"What do I do?" I abandoned all pretense of tragic humanity and plunged into personal sorrow.

"Don't cry," Jay said. "Unbutton two buttons. Just try it. Unbutton your top two buttons and hold your head up sometimes! And wash your hands. Like, for real, with a nailbrush."

He reminded me of Milton Erickson. I wondered whether my resistance to change was a product of my history, some sad admixture of fear of abandonment and training by the Hendersons, a rut from long habit, or an addiction.

I waited for him to ask me how Peter described him, but he never asked. (Peter had called him an artist trapped in the mind of a linebacker trapped in the body of a skater with the long legs of a eunuch who wanted to be trapped in the body of Lady Gaga.)

Jay also told me about his new plan for a dance project. There were no muscular or flexible dancers in his dance studies program, just a lot of part-time aficionados whose skills included walking in circles, and he was starting to feel at home. He wanted to outsource his eurythmy to a second dancer and concentrate on flamenco. The eurythmicist would spell his micro-poetry while he danced the corresponding emotion. It would look wonderful, because he would wear dapper matte black and stomp, while eurythmicists wore pastel silk muumuus draped with scarves and pattered around the stage like ghosts. He was looking for a collaborator online. He planned to meet some candidates as soon as college started up again.

———

The former literary-magazine staff met up after Christmas dinner, at Will's house, in its entirety this time.

Henry's mood was dour. His parents had moved into thin-walled condominiums that each cost half as much as the house where he grew up. Something about rage or adulthood had made his beard growth explode, and it was coming in kinky, causing abundant ingrown hairs. Fifi's apparent indifference to him was almost persuasive. Sitting in Mark's green suede recliner and compulsively petting its arms, she reacted to Jay's new information by remarking that his combination of flamenco and eurythmy could be unique, unless there were Waldorf schools in Spain, which of course there had to be. Henry interrupted her by snapping at Jay, "It needs to stop. If it ends up online, you'll have to quit school and change your name."

Jay defended himself, saying that communicating text through movement was an important dance experiment.

"Experiment?" Henry said. "Is there something new about what you're doing? What about sign language? Charades?"

Will said sternly, "New topic!"

Jay remained steadfast, because he believed in himself and his art. He had left the sheltering confines of high school without finding a new peer group, and his inner life had inflated until it took up all the space in his head. His epic-poet friend Rick was way too strange to slow him down, and Peter was too intensely interested in him, in his abstract way. That is, Peter's attention only encouraged him. He replied, "Those are merely based on English, but dance is a language in its own right."

Will grimaced, and Henry glared at Jay with obvious loathing. Fifi started talking about *The Sopranos*. She was good at remembering plots and entertained us all for a while by retelling them, like a bard. Then the conversation devolved into the minutiae of daily life, such as what the dorms were like at UCSD versus Yale.

I had nothing to contribute. Nothing in my life had changed, except for the advent of Peter, which I hoped to keep a secret. He had made me feel ashamed that nothing in my life had changed. Still, it was nice to see them all, as long as we stayed off the subject of ourselves.

The next time I visited Peter, in January, I drove him to Topanga State Park. We hiked uphill until we had a nice view of the ocean. Almost the whole time, he ranted about Jay in terms that would have made Jay want to crawl under a rock.

His criticisms revolved around a fact that was common knowledge: that Jay could not dance. That he danced like someone parodying flamenco as a joke. That far from garnering condemnation for racist appropriation of a "Gypsy" aesthetic, he was in danger of drawing even greater condemnation for the abjectness of his failure to appropriate it. Peter seemed unsure which was more horrifying in an Anglo-American of Russian extraction—competent or incompetent folklore of color—but he feared both. By taking his act public, Jay was putting himself at risk of summary social-media execution.

"The way his eyes dart from side to side," he said. "As if it were bharatanatyam, but in time with neither the music nor his own movements. He looks dissociated and panicked. It's like he's being abused onstage." He took a deep breath. "I mean sexually abused. It can't be deliberate. I can't believe he knows he's wincing like a five-year-old on his first date."

"His teacher can't see little details like that," I reminded him.

"Has anyone ever told him he might have an insoluble problem? It's like watching a machine malfunction. There's no communication without a common language, and what language is he even using? It's gibberish, and it's disturbing. It's powerful art, in its way, but I know it's not what he wants."

I remembered Henry's remarks, as well as thoughts I had entertained earlier on this very subject, but I said, "It's harshest when he looks like he's about to take a shit."

"You don't get it," he said. "Why would you? Your lives are so personal. Probably I've been damaged by wanting to be a public success. I self-censor. This view is amazing." He paused at a bend in the trail to squint up at the afternoon sun over the Pacific. "You and Jay live from the inside out. You're pure interiority. I had this idea that Californians would be superficial, but you're not superficial. You're inside-out outlaws! The uniformity—maybe you can't see it, because you see it all the time. There's no individuality on the surface of things here. It's the absence of a foundation of shared cultural modes. The impossibility of communication, because the culture is so new you can't even call it artificial. It's infancy. There's no society here. You're adrift in your solitary swaddling clothes, like impacted molars."

"You sound like Henry," I said. "He was bitching a lot about Jay at Christmas."

"That's the price I pay for coming to the West Coast," he said. "He's at Yale, firming up his standards, while I wriggle down into the dirt out here to get a worm's-eye view of zombie capitalism slouching toward In-N-Out Burger to be born."

"Eurythmy is an established way of spelling words," I protested. "It's cultural. Maybe it's not supposed to be expressive. It's like words on a page. It's marks you have to be able to read, like code. It would be like hating Jay's writing on account of his handwriting, when you can't read what he's saying."

"But who can? And tell me, Bran, is that what art is for?" He put a hand up to shade his eyes. "The sun up there, it's not *spelling* light. If someone's on fire inside—burning up—do you need a decoder to feel the warmth? Life is a burning fire, and art should be a burning fire. Can you feel it? We're both on fire, and what Jay's doing is cooling it off, tearing it down, dancing collapse and surrender and death."

I decided that this was not a hundred percent about Jay's dancing. I reached up for his hand. In return he gripped mine—crushingly, like a vise. He drew me toward him, twisting my arm behind my back, so that our faces were very close to each other. I felt my own heat blooming on my skin. He was hyperventilating. Leaning forward from the waist, I gave him a peck on the cheek, low down, almost on his neck—a quick peck, like a real chicken would. It was an attempt to indicate, in the only code I knew, that I was on fire.

He put both arms around me and pulled me very close, exhaling like a steam locomotive, with a heavy puffing sound. He clenched his teeth and closed his eyes tightly, as if he were trying to expel all the air in his body and seal the exits like a free diver. I gave him a better, warmer, more cautious kiss. We hovered as close as we could be, without skin contact, staring into each other's eyes. Our lips were just barely touching. Then he opened his mouth, moving his tongue against mine, to say, lisping slightly, "You should know I'm engaged."

I stiffened and said, "You're *what*?"

"I'm getting married." I leaned into him again, unable to give up the extremely strange thing I had believed, for a moment, was mine. "We can't be kissing anymore," he said mournfully. "I got engaged to somebody over Christmas."

I became conscious of my hands on his back and his penis against my pelvis and said, pulling away, "That's so fucked."

"So am I."

"What do you mean, 'fucked'? You could at least be happy."

"I've only known her for a few days. She's friends with my ex, who dumped me last year to go back to Brunei, but they were both in Boston for Christmas, and, I don't know, she comforted me. She's comforting." He turned to look at the sun again. Out in the ocean, a gray whale crested and rolled like an enormous slug. There was fear in his eyes. I could see that he had no idea what the whale was. "She didn't want to spend time alone with me until we were engaged."

"How does that even count? Were you drunk?"

"No," he said. "I don't drink. I had to formally ask for her dad's approval."

"That's so fucked," I repeated, like a malfunctioning machine.

He shrugged. "She might have the right idea. You can make plans for a marriage in the future, for after you get out of college, when you have time for stuff like that, and then until it happens you can focus on your work. That's the idea. You have no idea how ambitious I am for my career."

"Is she a college student?"

"She lives with her parents full time. She wants to be a housewife married to a professor like her dad. She'll make my life so much easier. She told me she wouldn't want any help with kids. She would want to raise them on her own, so I can do my work."

"That's fucking . . ." I wanted to say it was sexist bullshit for him to want kids someone else would raise, but I realized in time that running him down was crap tactics. I could not recall ever feeling any desire as strong as the need I felt at that moment to have him laugh at me and say his fiancée story was a mean joke.

"What was that thing in the water?" he asked. "Cthulhu? Mothra?"

"A gray whale," I said.

"It was hideous." He stared at the water, shading his eyes, clearly hoping to see it again.

"That's just how it looks from the outside," I said. "Under the blubber, it's super hot."

"Like you," he said. "I cannot *tell* you how much I would like to put my hands on you. To see you naked. I stumbled into an arranged marriage, Brunei-style, but even when I was holding you in my arms just now, I couldn't stop thinking how smart it was to get engaged to Yasira. You're not uncomplicated. But you know that."

"And she's simple, or what?"

"She's simple." He nodded. "I need simple things in my life. I'm sorry. I really am." He stepped back to the path and extended his hand in an invitation to continue walking.

"I hate you," I said. I lurched a half step toward him and a half step back. I stood like a dead cornstalk, wondering how I could possibly get any simpler, because I felt binary, like I was zero and he was one—that simple.

He circled, teetering a bit, to turn downhill and back toward my car. He held his hands out at waist level, as if he were dizzy in a dark place and feeling his way to keep from falling. He looked like he might faint.

I croaked, "Wait," and he waited.

When I got to him, I could see that he had been crying. We walked together in silence for a minute. He touched my hand again. I raised my head to make sure he saw my wet face. I unbuttoned two buttons, as if that would help him see my fucked heart. We stood on the trail and kissed open-mouthed, fiercely clutching at each other's hair.

We kissed like Roland blowing his horn at Roncesvalles, with desperation, yet no host of angels materialized to tell him it was okay to get buyer's remorse and ditch that girl. A couple coming up the hill interrupted us, and we started walking down again.

I drove him back to college in the middle of rush hour, suspecting myself of little blackouts. I could remember the left to get on the freeway in Santa Monica, but I had no memory of driving down the canyon, nor was I sure how exactly I dented my right rear fender backing up to a gas pump. Fortunately the surroundings were noisy—a penetrating dull roar coming off the PCH—and what I scraped was a concrete curb clad with thick steel. There was no reason for anyone to ask for my license, registration, or insurance.

had thought that Peter and I were over forever, but to my astonishment, yea, to the incredulous amazement of my puerile naïveté, he never missed a beat. A week later, he was up for another tense and exciting walk, with occasional brushing of hands against hands and a conversation that consisted of almost nothing but romantic double entendres.

We rambled through an open-air shopping mall, where there was neither privacy nor any real necessity to look where we were going, while he told me about fin-de-siècle Vienna. He said that to understand the penultimate turn of the century, I would have to read this one play by Arthur Schnitzler about a chain of people who all thought they were fucking superiors to get ahead, except that the chain went in a circle; plus the love poetry of Oscar Wilde; plus something involving the Greeks and matriarchy. The Olympian gods such as Zeus were shills for patriarchy, a stupid innovation. Before their advent, there reigned an interminable era during which no one had yet figured out that pregnancy involved sperm. In those endless days, women ruled the world. Only recently had science dethroned them. Before the discovery that men caused pregnancy, he would have been under no obligation to marry Yasira. She could have slept around, tended her kids, and let him live his life until he was torn apart by maenads. He talked a little about feminist authors for whom emancipated women would anchor matriarchal families, as with the old-school Greeks. Since society is no longer matriarchal, he told me, they will never stop complaining. He also told me more about Yasira. She was all done with junior college, where she had majored in swimming.

Our next walk had to be postponed because of all my overtime. But on the day Doug and Axel finally delivered the eight hundred bushes to the hospital in Bel Air, we met at a café on campus. There was something indiscreet about being so public—Jay might get jealous—but we both knew he was obsessed with creating his dance project. He barely had time for us anymore.

We talked about me. He demanded to know what was keeping me with the Hendersons. I told him about the eerie alternatives I had seen. Renting a place of my own, as he liked to suggest, would require a credit rating and a thousand dollars a month. "If it bothers you, I can move into your room," I concluded. "I'll get an air mattress."

"The dorm regulations wouldn't allow it," he said. "There are limits on how long visitors can stay. And what would you do in the summer?"

"Move to a homeless encampment." Even as I said it, I realized I might know a good one. Years before, I had seen a man living in the cab of a pickup truck at Entradero Park—a picturesque enclave with ball fields and a pond, up the hill in Torrance, surrounded by well-maintained single-family homes. "Wait," I said. "There's a park in Torrance I could move to."

"Oh, no. Don't say that. It makes you sound mentally unstable. Don't go doing things that make me want to diagnose you."

"I'm not kidding. I saw a guy living there once. An older guy. It might be safe. I should check it out."

"Bran," he said. "Do *not* move to a public park because I pressured you to leave the Hendersons. Just don't. I would feel so bad."

"How would it be your fault?" I said. "It's their fault. Let them feel bad! Let the Hendersons and my grandparents and my dad feel bad for once!"

"You need to take yourself more seriously," he said. "Your life is a precious gift. It's very precious to me, if not to you, and it's inextricably linked to your body, so your body needs to stay safe."

"Nobody is ever safe," I said. "Life is tragic, remember?"

"It doesn't have to be this tragic."

"So protect me," I said. "You could marry me tomorrow. They have married student housing."

"God," he said, turning away. "If you only knew."

"If I knew *what*?" I said. "All I know is, you're living like a monk—like a priest—living life like it's a booby prize, because you're engaged to this girl you don't know!"

He took his phone from his back pocket. "I want you to see a picture of Yasira," he said. He held the phone at me, arm straight. The photo depicted a rear view of a woman who was lying on an unmade bed, naked. He used his finger and thumb to zoom in on her perfectly smooth teardrop ass. He flipped to the next picture and I saw her beautiful face. In the next shot, she was wearing a tight blue dress of heavy silk, cut on the bias with a rippling thigh-high slit, and spike heels. She looked like a thousand-dollar call girl at her respectable best friend's wedding.

"Fuck," I said, hanging my head and clutching my flannel sleeves with both hands.

"I didn't sleep with her," he said. "I never asked for that picture." Showing me the phone again, he said, "This is her father." The man looked like a biker–bar bouncer—a three-hundred-pound thug with a BMI of thirty-six—in a slightly fuzzy three-piece suit with (to my mind) a telltale shoulder-holster bulge.

"He's a volunteer customs agent," I said. "His sidearm of choice is a ball-peen hammer."

"I wish," Peter said. "He's a Knight Commander of the Order of the British Empire, and a trustee of the Rhodes Trust. The one that picks Rhodes scholars. He's one of the top Chaucer experts in the world."

"And you're sure he's not bullshitting you?"

"He thinks I'm a suitable partner for his daughter."

"I should call him," I said. "I know you better than that already. You have a smooth surface because all the little gears are moving so fast, but it's an optical illusion, and when it breaks down, it's going to be debris all over the goddamn place!" I frowned, because it worked equally well as a description of myself.

"I love you," he said, putting one arm around my shoulders and hugging me. First jovially, then convulsively, then limply, then in the form of a tender caress all the way down my back.

I felt I was being fucked with, and I liked it a lot. Also that he was being fucked with and liked it a lot. We were doomed.

———

On the walk after that, I came out of my shell a little bit and educated him about the horticultural highlights of the UCLA campus. It was littered with valuable shrubs, rare saplings, and priceless vines, some well worth stealing. I said I hoped the Hendersons never got wind of them. Peter pointed out the security cameras and suggested I encourage them to show up and commit felonies. My life would be so much better when they were in jail.

I told him he knew too little about the nursery business. Bourdon Farms without Grandpa Larry would not be passed on to me, or even to Axel and Doug. There would be liens, debts, unwritten obligations. Someone else would move in. He proposed the Great Old Ones (e.g., Cthulhu, from the H. P. Lovecraft stories) as follow-up tenants and I said, "Something like that."

We walked for an hour until it was time to attend Jay's rehearsal. He had reserved a regular semiweekly slot—two hours on Monday and Friday evenings—in a mirrored dance studio in the student center and was working hard on his choreography. He wanted Peter's opinion. "Your *honest* opinion," he had emphasized.

This particular rehearsal turned out to be a semipublic event. There were two young boys there whom I had never seen before, both of them scruffy and grungy, and a girl named Casey, in denim overalls, whom I knew slightly because she had sat with us once in a food court, plus Jay's flamenco teacher, Loretta. I was so happy to see her again! It was wonderful to be able to introduce her to Peter after talking about her so much. He treated her with great courtesy. Until then I had never been sure he believed she was truly blind.

The boys were runaways whom Jay had made friends with. They plainly liked being inside a UCLA building. They whispered to each other while their backpacks clanked with many bottles. They did nothing untoward, sitting quietly on the floor.

Casey was a half-Brazilian materials-engineering major whose hobby was being in samba school. She wanted Jay to join her troupe, because they needed more men.

Also present, with several daintily dressed friends, was the eurythmy interpreter, Ashley, whom he had recruited to perform his poetry. This time it was a haiku that had been compressed to save letters. It went:

Surfer.
Light[ning]! Run [to] car.
Nude rain.

As a coda, she spelled this super-trendy smell Jay claimed everybody was into, "petrichor." The choreography kind of worked. The pounding of the thunder, the pattering of the rain, the naked surfers' joy in the raw power of nature, etc. If he had known how to dance, it could have been bearable.

The music was from a CD, but Loretta clapped along anyway. She was clearly satisfied with the castanets-and-tap-dancing angle and occasionally said, "*¡Olé!*" when he landed a stomping sequence. Another promising aspect was that the contrast to eurythmy was everything he had hoped for. Ashley wafted back and forth, her gestures ethereal but insistent, weightless as a real dancer. But Jay! Jay.

Somewhere in the middle, the runaways stood up and left. Casey focused her eyes exclusively on Ashley while I kept track of Jay. Peter's eyes were slits, but I could see that they were open. When it was over, he clapped and said, still clapping, "I'm reexamining my conviction that there is no role for censorship in art."

Loretta said, "Off your high horse, college boy. Have you been to Andalucía? It's full of lousy dancers. That's not what folk dance is about. I gather your jaded eyes have never seen anything but canonic art and glossy pop stars."

"I wasn't saying it wasn't excellent," Peter said, turning to her attentively. "Just that he'll go down in flames online for being unwittingly hilarious, and maybe worse."

"That's what art is about," she replied. "Taking risks."

Jay came up to us with Ashley. He was still out of breath. "You were absolutely wonderful, Ashley, darling," Loretta said.

Ashley shot a sidelong look at Jay and whispered, "Isn't she blind?"

"I can see colors and motion enough to drive a car," she said. "I could see your movements better than anything I've seen in years. Bravo!"

"Thank you," Ashley said, moving away to talk with her anthroposophist pals.

"How was I?" Jay asked Loretta.

"I'm told your facial expressions need work," she said, looking at Peter. "They're distracting to our friend Peter."

I said, "He's too mean for a rehearsal, but there's something about flamenco that you're not getting right."

"Duende deficit," Peter said.

Casey said, in the chipper tones of a marketer, "You should join our samba school! Zero duende required!"

"That's something of a brilliant idea," Loretta said.

"But samba's not a tool I need," Jay said. "It's about joie de vivre or something, and I want to tell stories."

"You should take a kathak course at the Indian community center," Peter suggested. "It's like shorthand eurythmy from Rajasthan. You can dance and tell stories at the same time without implicating other people, and the outfits are great. So is the music."

"You don't get it," Jay said. "I want to tell stories with duende, not cute sagas."

"So what is duende?" Casey asked. "Besides the opposite of enjoying life."

"Indefinable and incommensurable," Loretta said. "You either have it or you don't. It's in your blood, like soul and rhythm for Black people. That's the theory."

Casey said, "I didn't come here to be subjected to microaggressions from some old white woman."

Loretta turned toward her in an openly aggressive posture—*sentada*, with her arms crossed at waist level, vaguely suggesting kung fu—and said, "Who you calling old?" For the record, she was eighty-one.

"Older white woman," Casey corrected herself.

"I'm a quarter Native American," Loretta retorted, raising her hands to chest level and snapping her fingers.

Peter said, "Oh, shit."

I said, "Loretta, are you sure? Because that's what Grandpa Larry's friends all say."

"No, I'm pretty sure," she said, dropping her hands. She added, "My grandma said she met a gorgeous Indian fishing and never knew his name, and that's why my mom was called Shasta, after the mountain."

"Cool name," I said.

"But Casey, sweetie"—she turned to Casey, who was suddenly filming her—"I didn't mean to offend you. If I didn't think dancing could be taught, I'd retire and go back to the go-go clubs. Men are so freaking strange, I'm sure some place would take me. I'm being offensive again. But I'm thinking you're a lesbian? Are you not a lesbian? I can't see you very well, but I thought—"

Casey, as she stormed off, called us all crazy. Like the rough-sleeping runaway boys and Ashley and her friends, I never saw her again.

As we walked across campus to get coffee, Jay and Peter argued the duende issue at length. Peter suggested that Jay had never experienced flamenco's foundational emotion, jealousy. Jay's response was, "Dude goes off and gets engaged to some rando over Christmas for no reason and thinks I don't know what it means to be jealous. Yeah, right!"

I envied Jay. Jealousy was a common enough emotion, to which uncomplicated people like me were entitled, but I was not feeling it. As Peter had explained it, he had due cause and every right to marry Yasira. I was a distant second, shut out from the pole position from birth. The feeling felt familiar, right, and true. Renunciation was dignified, stoical, and tragically human. Somehow he had managed to convince me that humility was the sexiest move available, which was insane. "I need to be more jealous," I said.

"No one needs to feel emotions to perform them," Loretta said, apparently thinking I meant to impugn my own flamenco dancing. "Performance shouldn't be that subtle."

"The best performance is no performance at all," Peter said. "Like Kleist said, the perfect dancer is a marionette."

"Please explain," Loretta said.

"Submitting to gravity makes you graceful. That's all duende is, that kind of feral authenticity. Surrender. But only to gravity. Jay dances like he's surrendering to everything. His own body, or his mind. That's what makes it so hellish. Like the twitching of souls in hell, where the impetus comes from below, from inside, like pain. Like a surrender to pain. It's a higher-order passivity, what he's doing. He's actively dancing out submission to metaphysical gravity—to entropy—I need to think about this."

"You make me sound like the most interesting dancer ever," Jay said.

Jay and Ashley never performed their number in public, because the dress rehearsal went viral. Maybe if he had not jumped up and down quite so much, or if his boots had been less pointy, or he had not looked quite so bowlegged? Recorded as a matter of routine by the university media department, the video created the impression that he had crashed a eurythmy performance as a prank.

Ashley disliked being laughed at by thousands of strangers. So that was that—no more collaboration.

For well over twenty-four hours, Jay was hounded by trolls and targeted for expulsion by the Romany Student Association, a fictional social-media account hastily concocted by someone in England.

He would have been suicidal all day and night if not for Peter. Every time some hater's contumely had him working himself into a state, it would appear in his email inbox as a screenshot, its logical and aesthetic inadequacies tallied and annotated. He might have been canceled to the world, but Peter's was the opinion he cared about.

He made a strategic retreat from social media into reality. In three-dimensional meatspace, he was still invisible. His habits and appearance in real life bore no resemblance to those onstage. As forced and stilted as his dancing was, so casual and cavalier was his way of loping around campus. Since the events of seventh grade, he had never worn his boots outside rehearsal.

The storm raged, died down, and was forgotten. There had been no aggrieved parties but God (Peter assured him that his dancing was an offense against God) and idle gawkers as far away as Tasmania.

After years of cajoling individuals to listen to his poems or watch him dance, Jay had been a little shocked by the readiness of the masses to watch a video clip over and over. But only because he had been repressing a stark truth: that he himself had read several books in his life, attended a few dance performances, and consumed two to ten hours of audiovisual media nearly every day since before he could walk. He announced his intention to transfer to UCLA's film school at the earliest opportunity. He had already registered and paid the deposit for an intensive flamenco summer course in Málaga, Spain, but he let it ride, saying, "Who knows. I might learn to dance."

His insight into his true passion (film) had arisen, he said, not from his worthless college courses, but via Socratic dialogue with Peter. He had learned all he needed to know—that life should be looked in the face, with uncompromising honesty— and if he was at a loss on any given aspect, he could always ask Peter.

Because I could catch Peter's drift faster than Jay, I fancied myself more intelligent. Over instant coffee in his dorm room, Peter disabused me of that notion. "You don't have an analytic mind," he said. "You're just a rigorous paranoiac." He claimed that the educated intelligentsia do not occupy an enviable position. They are parasites on the creative class, to which I would soon belong. Where he was destined to spend his life critiquing people like me, I would spend mine inventing things that had never before existed, embodying the essence of tragic humanity while he served as my humble mirror.

I asked whether he was calling me stupid or crazy or both.

"Genius is creative genius, which is insanity," he said. "There's no other kind. There are no stories without paranoia." I opened my mouth to pose the question again and he said, "I'll put it like this. It's insane to think art matters, and you're far from stupid." He claimed that I could make a good living writing popular fiction or screenplays, and if the idea terrified me, all the better. "Women artists traditionally shelter behind the mask of genre," he said. "You're a woman, the real deal, the kind they don't make anymore. You have the horizons of Emily Dickinson. That's a limitation you can turn into serious cash."

I demanded details.

"Murder mysteries, for instance," he said. "People die under questionable circumstances in real life all the time, and the police don't investigate. Nobody cares. But in the imaginary, humans are paranoid and persistent, instead of absentminded and apathetic, and each and every unavenged corpse stops the world in its tracks until we find its killer, with the help of the nonviolent priestly ascetics of law enforcement, who can even be elderly women, Miss Marple et cetera. The world doesn't cohere on its own. It takes paranoia to connect the dots. Your mental life takes place in that kind of fictional aesthetic dream-time. It's a limitation, not a disadvantage."

When I said that I finally saw what he meant, he replied, "I could be wrong. It's a merciless critique, but it's fictitious to the extent that I'm making it up."

He went to his shelves and took down a battered paper-back copy of *Monster,* by John Gregory Dunne. Like many of his books, it had been around the block and was full of other people's highlighter and pencil marks. "You can keep this," he said, handing it to me. "It's about the experience of screenwriting. Dunne gets persecuted in absentia by this evil producer he wants to work for. It's a lot like *The Castle.* You should write movie scripts and make money. Jay's going to be a producer, and he'll help you out. Are you surprised? His family is so rich. He's not going to be the kind of guy who rings doorbells looking for work. He's going to invest for a living. Did you not know that? He'll make a killing. His taste is so—plebeian."

Henry came home from Yale for spring break. It had been his idea to reserve a table for lunch at the Kettle on Saturday, with plans to stroll the pier and play some vintage games at a video arcade. The Kettle was not the cheapest place. But gas was cheap, and my car got me to Pasadena to see my grandparents on a regular basis, so I had several twenty-dollar bills saved up. When I got to the restaurant, he looked up from his conversation with Fifi and said, "You monster."

Neither smiled. His stodgy clothes looked brand new and stiff, and so did hers—a white cotton blouse fuzzed up with pulse warmers made of sage-green felt. They both looked odd and a bit stern, as if they were celebrating Lent as a time of atonement.

I said hello to the two of them and asked, "Where are Will and Jay?"

"You know what I'm talking about," Henry said. "Jay's friend Peter. What do you think you're doing?" He held up his menu like a riot shield to ward me off, propping it vertically on the table.

"What are you talking about?"

"Bran."

"No hard feelings, Bran," Fifi said. "I had to tell him."

"What about?"

"That shit bugs me! You know what I mean."

I had not sat down. I was still standing there in the aisle, blocking busy waiters' paths around the counter and toward the rear of the restaurant, and I had the feeling that Henry and Fifi had joined forces and desired immediate capitulation. I folded my arms and leaned forward to whisper, "Had to tell Henry what? Because I literally do not know."

Henry said, "Peter is engaged."

I said, "So?"

They looked at me in silence, and Fifi said, "Sit down."

"No. Not until you tell me what you're accusing me of."

"Take a wild guess," Henry said.

It was finally obvious to me what they meant. "You wish," I said. "But there is nothing between us. Nothing."

Fifi frowned. If there was nothing, she had trafficked in rumor, and we both knew that Henry regarded himself as an ethical person with a right to sit in judgment because he knew first aid. She had not been a gossip in high school. Back when we all immediately knew the least little thing that happened to any of the others, there was no need for it.

But I had never been sexually active. Not in the least and not with anyone, least of all Peter.

Who had prompted her line of thought? It could only have been Jay, who just then showed up with Will. They had come early to make sure they found parking, gone walking on the beach, and spent the next twenty minutes scraping tar off their feet with paper towels and baby oil from a surf shop.

I sat down next to Fifi to make room for them. The booth squeaked as she slid away from me. They both hugged Henry, whom they had not seen in months. Jay sat across from me and said eagerly, "Have you heard from Peter? Is he in Maine?"

"I guess so," I said. "I don't know. We're not as close as some people think."

Jay exchanged glances with Fifi. "Come on, Bran," he said. "It needs to be in the open, so we can talk about it."

"It does not," I said. "There is nothing between us that does not belong between us. Everything about our friendship is private. It's not yours to talk about."

"Are you sure? He talks to me about you all the time," Jay said.

"You're lying. You lied to Fifi, and she made Henry think I'm a bad person."

"Lying about what?"

"That I'm sleeping with him or something."

"He said he's in love with you. Why would I lie about that? It's too crazy!"

I was not thrilled to hear this fresh tidbit from Jay in such a context. I blinked hard.

"Either way, he's engaged to somebody else," Henry said.

"You should not be spending hours alone with this guy in his dorm room."

"You need to give him space," Fifi said.

"I would want you to do the same for me," Henry said.

"You're all insane," I said. "What am I now, a femme fatale? A witch, and he's an innocent child and I cast a spell? Or what? That's it. You think I bewitched him, because he'd have to be crazy to love me."

"But, Bran," Fifi said. She stroked my forearm with her closed fist. "He's marrying Yasira. What he feels for you is not love. He's using you. You need to get out of this mess. We want to help."

"I don't want out," I said. "We're friends, and I don't want to talk about it. I want waffles with syrup and sausage patties."

"Are you pregnant?"

I looked at Fifi long and hard. It was suddenly apparent to me that she must be engaged to Henry.

"What happens in Bran stays in Bran," Henry quipped.

"Don't be crude," Fifi said.

Will said, "Stop being mean to Bran, before she starts crying. You're going to get us thrown out of here, and I'm hungry."

"Peter said you almost went all the way," Jay said, addressing me.

The statement seemed designed to intimidate me, so that my confession would be their program of lunchtime entertainment. But I was unable to be submissive where Peter was concerned.

"Jay's going to Málaga," I said, in a deft change of subject.

I could retail numerous aspects of his plan, from the name of the summer flamenco academy to the difficult choice he was forced to make among a host family option, an evening language course that provided apartment referrals, and university student housing.

He soon hijacked the discourse to embroider it with hopes and dreams. Fifi opined that he would roast alive.

"On the *beach*," Jay clarified.

"Surrounded by hot Spanish dudes," Will said.

"You mean drunken British dudes," Henry said.

"I'll be with flamenco people all the time," Jay said. "It's an immersion program. If I can't dance after two months in Málaga, I swear I'll give it up."

"I'm trying to imagine flamenco on a beach," Henry said.

"It's quieter," I said.

I stayed in the conversation without saying much. The little wheels in my head turned faster and faster, wondering whether Peter wanted me to get him drunk and jump him. If we had sex, he would tell Yasira, and she would break it off. I did not know how people have sex and wondered whether he knew.

CHAPTER SIX

The next time I visited Peter alone in his room, he immediately embarked upon a long lamentation at having chained himself to Yasira. He talked and I listened, as passive as a fly on the wall. Having formally requested her hand in marriage from her father at Christmas so that they could talk unchaperoned, he had learned too late that this made him a member of an extended family in which he was expected to take a heartfelt interest. He had been planning over spring break to write a scholarly article for publication, but her family had co-opted all his spare time. Maybe he could have tolerated it if it had involved hours alone with her, but they were never alone together. He had discussed politics with her right-wing aunt and uncle and been made to view his late future grandfather-in-law's collection of rare watches and pick the one he would like best as a wedding present. She had told him that it would be like this only until they were married, their engagement was announced at a party, or they eloped. She said this in front of her mother, who laughed and said she and Yasira's father had escaped similar family pressures by eloping, and that she would fully understand if Peter and Yasira chose to get married right away.

The stress had given him acne. His perfect skin was marred

with a raised pattern of angry red dots. I put my arms around him. There was no response. He slumped into a heap, his mottled face expressionless. He was like a half-inflated football waiting to be drop-kicked off the field. He would not leave the game under his own power. He seemed inaccessible, unavailable, not himself, as if she had locked him in a dark tower.

I asked him what his parents thought of the Yasira thing, hoping they were already campaigning actively against his plans.

"They're fine with it," he said. "They never expected me to end up with such a nice girl."

"Oh," I said, imagining Yasira had spent some weekend at his family home in Maine.

"There are things you don't know about me," he said. "Things nobody knows except my parents. Their expectations for me aren't super high."

"Whatever you did, it can't be bad," I said. "Because whoever you were before, you're you now."

"You're the most—I mean the only—nonjudgmental person I ever met," he said. It was hard to tell whether he thought it mattered. "Maybe because you were socialized at Bourdon Farms. I seldom have the feeling I'm disappointing you. Your expectations are even lower than theirs."

"Did you kill somebody?"

"It was purely self-destructive behavior. I didn't do anything to anyone."

"You mean like drugs?"

"Totally like drugs."

As he had predicted, I failed to look upset. I also failed to see what he was worried about. I had the impression, based on Jay's anecdotes, that drugs on college campuses were routine, if not a requirement. MDMA was not considered a drug in its own right; it was a thing you took to stay alert while drinking. People did lines of ketamine to counteract the effect of too many lines of cocaine. Peter had merely mixed codeine with Mahler and progressed to oxycodone with Bruckner, spending an entire summer in his room.

He explained that Rhodes scholars and the like are not typically drawn from the ranks of those in recovery. It was no longer possible or permissible to crash and burn and emerge with a blank slate. Once a narcoholic, always a narcoholic. Even fifteen-year-olds felt pressure to join the recovery community online before it found and exposed them. He had never gone public, and thus was vulnerable to blackmail.

"The thing is," he said, "I was so sneaky that nobody at my school found out. It was just my parents and the rehab clinic. But I could never tell Yasira. It might get back to her dad."

"I don't get it," I said. "You don't trust her, but you want to marry her?"

"She's supremely loyal to family. If you're going to get married, that's the kind of person you would want. Anybody else might give up on you. A traditional marriage is not based on sex. Like Guattari says, 'Orgasm is another overblown notion whose ravages are incalculable.' Ideally it's a stable, mutually advantageous business arrangement. She wants to be supported, and in exchange she'll give me the freedom to spend my professional career doing what I want."

I could feel the intensity of the moment peeling away to expose an ugly vapidity I wanted nothing to do with. I said, "That sounds totally medieval. And guys in traditional marriages can always do whatever they want. There's a double standard." There was no need for me to go back to the medieval era for examples; I only had to look at my father and Doug.

"Obviously," he said. "Monogamous marriage was never intended to be faithful. Maybe that's why I wanted it in the first place. For us."

"Huh? What?"

"For us. Our affair. Tristan and Iseult."

"On drugs," I said, thinking of the love potion that brought them together. I wished I had one. It would have helped me concentrate.

He shook his head and said, "When I'm with you, I forget about drugs." He enfolded me in a bear hug and kissed me on the mouth.

I did not resist, though I was being fucked with so, so bad. He had managed to make kissing a pimply English major in a dorm seem sublimely erotic and dangerous—is that not genius?

"I'm fated to marry the other Iseult," he added. "Iseult of the White Hands." He looked down at my hands (scarred, sun-tanned, calloused, scabby) and let them fall.

All was preordained lunacy. I left elated, walking on air.

Our next walk, back in the hilly park, was largely devoted to a monologue in which he outlined Edward Said's *Orientalism* and detailed the many ways in which his plans for Yasira violated contemporary ethical norms. "Heterosexuality is a form of orientalism," he said. "Or is it vice versa?" He took Kafka, Buber, and Lévinas to task for regarding the Other as inscrutable while declaring his utter ignorance of Yasira. "I feel I know her intimately," he said, "an obvious impossibility, an endocrine artifact, and, at the same time, that no amount of intimacy could reduce my alienation." He compared me to her in a way that made me struggle to keep quiet. "Your beauty," he said, reaching over—we were sitting facing each other side-saddle on a concrete retaining wall—to gather my hair at the back of my neck and expose my face, "is as coincidental as her wealth and influence. Hers is the product of thousands of years of refinement by a polygamous economic elite, and yours is a freak of biology." He was definitely plotting to drive me out of my mind.

"I'm so in love with you," I said, very much in the manner of a drunk person saying, "I'm drunk."

"I'm well aware of that," he said. "It's dangerous for both of us. It's one of the reasons I applied for a transfer to Harvard. They don't take many transfer students, but Yasira's dad thinks he can get me in."

"What the *actual fuck*? Isn't that in Boston?"

"It's a more reputable college, with an excellent comparative literature program. I should have gone there to begin with."

He began to break apart in my head, losing the illusory coherence lent him by my desire—my paranoid invocations of love.

"I might not get in," he added. "Supposedly they start notifying people in May, but I haven't heard anything yet. Don't panic. I might be in L.A. for three more years."

"You are—you are—" I could not think of anything to add. He put his hand to the side of my face and stroked my hair back with a look of bemused tolerance. I lowered my eyes and said, "Uh-huh. Okay, then."

———

The live-privet-topiary business turned out to be a license to print money, none of which accrued to me. In addition to the usual middlemen—the Hendersons—even Eric and Roger were dressing well and drinking expensive liquor.

They threw a massive Memorial Day barbecue, with five kegs, hundreds of pounds of chicken, and a sound system on a truck bed, for everyone we knew and the local Baoulé community. I invited all my friends at the last minute, after the party started and I realized that Grandpa Larry's friends would be outnumbered by the Ivorians, but none of them came.

I was morosely certain that the whole thing had been financed by the sad fact that the value added every time I turned a six-foot bush into a cone with a ball on top was around $225. I drank beer and danced barefoot with a group of West African moms, staring at the ground.

Eventually I was drunk enough to break out of my accustomed habits of thought and have an epiphany: that I could make a living doing yard work if I lived in my car.

It was too small to put a lawn mower inside, but not everybody had a lawn. Lots of people had rock gardens instead, and they still needed their trees and shrubs trimmed. I could rake their leaves. A hedge trimmer and a rake would fit in my car, no problem. I could go door-to-door offering my services, and a certain number of people would say yes, given my race, gender, and size privilege, since I would not require payment up front or access to the house. If they stiffed me, I would be making no worse money than with the Hendersons. I could eat at a good *taquería* every day. I could walk to the ocean every morning and swim to keep clean. Redondo Beach had a park with a campground. I could sneak in and use the showers. Peter could get all worked up worrying about me, and I could reassure him and not be believed, and he could fret and hug and touch me as if his caresses were solely paternal in nature, practice sessions for the paterfamilias job he had lined up down the road.

Around this time I became aware that Grandpa Larry and several friends of his were standing on the margins of the dance floor area, clapping their hands and chanting, "Take it off!" I looked around. None of the other women were stripping or appeared to be thinking even remotely about stripping. People were exiting the dance floor area at speed, leaving me alone.

Naturally I followed them, but I got pushed back into the center of a circle, with friends of Grandpa Larry's plucking at my shirt. "Show us your tits!" his friend Wayland said, pulling my shirttails up. Wayland was about forty-five and regarded himself as the last living exemplar of 1950s "greaser" culture. Another friend of theirs, Country, who used "country" as an adjective to describe himself and rode around on a chopper with chaps on, slapped Wayland's hands away from me and said, "She's not yours yet. Go ahead and let Larry auction her."

I yelled and flailed like somebody with no sense of humor, trying to push through an immovable wall of men. It was hard to be louder than the music, but eventually Eric came over to see who was spoiling his party. When he saw who it was, he went to get Axel, who broke up the fight. He kept telling me, "Ignore these guys. They're joking. They're kidding." They were still hooting and demanding I show them my tits, as a joke. I was out of breath and had lost some buttons. When we got clear of the crowd, I broke away from Axel and ran.

At first I ran straight north, toward Peter's room. I would have crawled there over broken glass. I would never go back to the Hendersons, because there was no need. All my valuables were in my pants pockets, even my car keys, reminding me that I had run right past my own car. I did not want to turn around and sneak back up the driveway to get it. I could see headlights leaving the party—single headlights, double, jeep headlights in close-set pairs, night-hunting arrays over the cabs of pickups. Maybe they were all heading home, or maybe Grandpa Larry's friends had formed a posse to bring me back, as a kindness toward one proven too vulnerable to have a sense of humor.

Remembering, as my breathing slowed, that Peter's room was twenty miles away in Westwood, I decided to run toward the bus stop instead. But it was after midnight, there were no more buses, and I had not yet run far enough.

I picked a new destination, Will's house, about a mile away—enough to wear me out—and ten minutes later was ringing the doorbell.

Mark let me in, saying, "Bran! What are you doing here? Did something happen? Are you okay?"

Susan came downstairs in a nightgown and bathrobe with her glasses on, looking more concerned with every step. She waved her husband away and whispered, "Do we need to go to the hospital?" She obviously thought I looked so not-okay that the only possible explanation was sexualized violence.

I knew she was right, but I did my best to calm her and convince her that nothing had happened. Things had gotten out of hand at a party, I had gotten groped, but I was all right, if dusty.

"Are you absolutely sure?" she said. "I shouldn't even let you take a shower, if there might be evidence—you know—if a crime has been committed—"

I assured her that no sex crime had occurred. I swore it up and down.

She said I should wash up while she got me an ice pack and readied the guest room. Through the bathroom door, while I stood staring into the mirror at the blood under my nose and on my shirt and at what looked like an incipient black eye—when did I get it? I absolutely did not remember getting hit—I could hear the most beautiful sound: Will's father, Mark, raising his voice, talking about that motherfucker Larry Henderson and his piece-of-shit son.

The next day they went to work and I was afraid to leave the house. I stayed in pajamas all day—striped flannel ones that belonged to Will—watching TV with my hand on the dog Lionel's head. While I slept, they had relieved me of my clothes, possibly with the aim of keeping me in the house; my money and phone were on the bedside table when I woke up, but everything I had been wearing was somewhere in the laundry. I ate cookies and made sandwiches with cold cuts and waited for them to get home safe. The closest I came to going outside was letting Lionel out the back door. I feared that if I showed myself out front, the Hendersons would drag me home to work and punish them for giving quarter to a fugitive. I drank a quart of orange juice and a quart of chocolate milk.

In the evening, they brought me my car. Susan had taken my keys out of my pants without asking my permission.

After work, instead of coming straight home, they had met up at a coffee shop, and she had driven Mark in her big white Avalon (full-size Toyota sedan) to Bourdon Farms to steal the

Mazda. Either no one noticed, which was hardly likely, or a choice was made not to intervene, or they lied to me when they said there was no confrontation. I think the Hendersons watched the car leave and said something to the effect of "Good riddance." In financial terms, it was worthless. A sexually taboo female servant was similarly expendable. My strength was limited. My skills could be learned. My departure freed up space in the house.

Mark's description of the events conveyed dismay at not having had an opportunity to make a stand. Somehow he seemed certain he would not get shot, despite marching into the Bourdon Farms compound to remove a vehicle. Apparently he knew that nobody there wanted the authorities poking around.

They put me in Mark's clothes, which fit better than Axel's. He was a petite guy, my height, with narrow shoulders, so on me they were capacious without getting in the way. He offered me jeans he said were too faded for work, even for casual Fridays. He professed to be done with patterned shirts and dark colors forever, until I felt emboldened to accept his Black Watch and Campbell plaids. Susan found me an unopened package of somewhat oversize underwear. Her socks looked tiny to me—I had never worn stretchy women's socks—so they gave me some of his.

Over dinner, she said, "What are we going to do with you? You should be in college."

I claimed that I could never get in.

"You have an inflated idea of what's required," Mark said. "Will and his friends were competing with thousands of other eager beavers to get into the fanciest places, and only Henry made it. Good for Henry, but it's not actually necessary to go to Yale. I went to Michigan State."

"Every college costs money," I said. "I have zero money."

"I know you have a father somewhere," he said. "Maybe I can help. I'm a lawyer."

"I don't want to go to college," I said. "I have this idea of offering landscaping services. I can live in my car. I'll save up and get my own place. It's good money."

"This is your life's dream?" he said. "You're a little too young to be compromising on career goals. You want to be fifty and mowing lawns?"

"No," I admitted. "But it's realistic."

"And if you had your choice of any job in the world? Maybe veterinary assistant? You get along great with Lionel."

For a moment I thought he had a point, but a vision of Peter gave me courage, and I said, "Well, I had this idea of being a screenwriter. If I had a computer, I could write screenplays. Do you remember Peter? He gave me a book about screenwriting."

"You look like a writer," Susan said. "You always have."

"Except for the shiner," Mark said.

"No, that's typical writer," she said. "They're always pissing people off."

Mark told a funny story about his work. He was defending an eighteen-year-old who had fatally shot a woman in plain view of about twenty people in Redondo Beach. He was roller skating down the ramp from the parking lot to the beachfront trail. The victim had stopped to talk to a friend, both pushing strollers, and they were blocking the entire ramp. No one could get past the enormous strollers. In the ensuing argument, the victim used the N-word. The defendant placed great stock in his moral virtue and always carried a handgun in case he needed to teach someone a lesson. It was plain that he was lucidly psychotic and would be in prison until the sun burned out. He was the person the Fifth Amendment was created to protect. If he could manage to look sheepish in court, he might be eligible for parole in thirty-five years, but he was only interested in getting Mark to agree that use of the N-word is unforgivable, and Mark had to agree. "You can use this storyline in your screenplay, but I want royalties," he concluded.

Over dessert, I asked whether they knew that I had maternal grandparents in Pasadena. "I should call them," I said. "They might let me stay there for a week."

"It's your choice, but you're very welcome to stay here," Susan said. "We have plenty of room, and you look like you need a vacation."

"Ditto," Mark said. "I never saw a kid look so tired."

I recalled that my grandparents had not asked me to stay overnight since I was ten, and my head inclined forward until my hair hid my face. "I'm exhausted," I said, and went upstairs to bed.

The next morning, before she went to the clinic, Susan brought me an old smartphone and an old laptop. Ecologically minded people never throw those things away, because of the heavy metals and poisons. She and Mark had collections reaching back to the nineties.

The laptop looked pretty new to me—a lightweight and silvery Apple. I said I had never used an Apple, and she said I would get used to it. She asked what my screenplay was about, and I said I didn't know. She told me to take my time brainstorming and make myself at home.

I felt so lucky to have gotten to know her before I was all grown up and dripping blood. Outwardly, I was someone she would probably expect to empty every bottle and wallet in the house. But she could see my inner child.

I made myself a foot-deep bubble bath and spent an hour in there. I spent most of the rest of the day doing things like massaging my toes and lying around on top of the bedspread, patting the tops of my feet affectionately and twisting my hair into knots. It was my way of doing nothing. I was so used to working that I needed to move my hands. I tried masturbating, but instead of reminding me of Peter, it reminded me of lying in my cot at Bourdon Farms with the TV blaring two rooms away through the wall, so I stopped. They had magazines like *The New Yorker* and *The Atlantic* in a rack in the living room, so I brought some upstairs to read.

Around four p.m., I got up, put on a bathrobe over my PJs, and went downstairs to make dinner for them as a surprise. They had all the ingredients for scalloped potatoes au gratin, a labor-intensive dish Susan had taught me how to make. After putting the casserole in the oven, I sent a monosyllabic text to Jay ("Hey").

He wrote back to say he was still mad about Peter.

His ignorance of my doings gave me a feeling of power. I had finally left Bourdon Farms, I was wearing Will's pajamas, I was—for the moment—the most novel and interesting thing in all of L.A., and all he could remember was that we had fought about Peter.

I assumed he meant "still mad" as in angry that I had corrupted Peter's innocence with my sexual mayhem or whatever, so I planned to rebuke him with charges of orientalism. I texted back, "What did he do now."

Immediately my phone rang. It turned out Jay meant that he despaired of getting through the summer in Málaga without Peter. He was crazy about Peter. He would have talked to a rock, if it would have talked to him about Peter.

He and I had not communicated since the scene at the Kettle. He had heard from Rick that Peter was planning to see Yasira over the summer. This would involve long connecting flights to Bandar Seri Begawan, even though her whole family lived in Wellesley and Cambridge, a couple of hours by car from his home in Maine. He would be joining the ceremonial pilgrimage they made every year to visit the graves of their ancestors in Brunei and certain bank accounts in Singapore. "Do you think I could talk him into stopping over in Málaga?" Jay pleaded. "What would you say to convince him, if you were me?"

"Is it on the way?" I asked. I was truly not sure.

"Brunei is on the exact opposite side of the earth from Maine," he said. "So basically it's his decision which way he goes."

I pointed out that he could visit L.A. heading out, and Málaga on the flipside.

"But he's going to Oxford!" Jay wailed. "Her uncle is meeting him there!"

If he was that upset about a few days in Oxford, he was surely unaware that Peter had applied to finish college in Massachusetts. I changed the subject to my own life—not the sad events of the party, but the saintliness of Susan and Mark. He screeched in celebration. He could not emphasize enough how long he had waited for this moment.

I was surprised. Since the arrangement was temporary, or at least not permanent—possibly very temporary; there had been no explicit discussion; Susan treated me like one recently bereaved—it had not crossed my mind that I might have escaped Bourdon Farms forever. The Susan-and-Mark inter-regnum felt like a sleepover. It was definitely not going to last past the day Will came home from UCSD for the summer. As it stood, I could almost argue that I was doing them a favor, con-soling the empty-nesters, but not with their son around. When he arrived, I would have to find someplace else to go. Since I could not think of a place that would take me rent-free except for Bourdon Farms, I would go home.

I ended up eating a lot of scalloped potatoes, since they came home only briefly before going out to dinner with friends. They were such nice people that they each ate a little bowl of my creation as an appetizer and snack. Mark said it might be hours before they got any real food at the fancy restaurant, where all the dishes took the form of ping-pong balls, strings, and shav-ing cream.

CHAPTER SEVEN

By the time Will showed up in mid-June, two weeks after me, I had been given leather sandals (Timberlands from the internet), but I had not set foot off his parents' property since my arrival. Whatever his parents told him, it made him casual and charitable about my taking up space in his house. He would be there only for a week before flying off to a biological station in Paraguay.

To my surprise, his visit was not spent in reliving the social scenes of high school. Henry was lingering in New Haven; they would miss each other by several days. Jay's obsession with Peter annoyed Will no end, and he was also avoiding Fifi, who talked about nothing but her schemes to get Henry back, if not in so many words. He spent hours texting and video-chatting with new friends from college. Two of them lived in L.A., in upscale sections with sidewalk cafés, so he drove us north to meet them. Riding in his car was like wearing a disguise, so I was nervous, but not afraid. It felt good to leave Torrance.

Neither friend struck me as remarkable, but they shared his newfound interest in tropical bugs. The bearded boy, Dante, also loved birds, and the tall girl, Louisa, also loved monkeys, but the three agreed that insects were the most fascinating and important of all. With their professor and two other students, they would be in Paraguay for nine weeks, collecting flies that lived in bromeliads. Dante was an experienced climber and archer and would ascend a hundred feet to the forest canopy using a bow and arrow and ropes. Louisa had begun gaining experience as a taxonomist in high school and had worked training AIs to classify specimens. Will was good at flying drones. I had nothing to contribute to their conversation. It was like watching coconspirators in a heist movie about stealing insects from the Death Star. The region was overrun with drug smugglers and human traffickers. They would have to move fast and watch their backs. There had been kidnappings. Not a lot of kidnappings, but historically, there had been kidnappings. They discussed how to behave when kidnapped, and how to take cover under fire.

I vicariously enjoyed their vicarious glamour, but the feeling of being truly impressed never came. I knew Will's parents too well by then. If the Paraguay plan had been dangerous, they would have found means of influencing him to do something else.

After he left, Susan took me to the public library to get a card. Nothing scary about that. The danger of seeing Hendersons at the library was nil. She pretended to be my mom, and it was the simplest thing. I checked out two Steinbeck novels and a book about screenwriting. Then we went grocery shopping at the big organic supermarket, another Henderson-free zone.

I learned that if I paid a little attention to what I was doing, I could exist in a parallel Torrance entirely free of Hendersons. I texted Peter, who replied, "China Miéville, The City & the City," followed by "No not rly for you. Murder mystery."

I finally called Grandma Tessa, who expressed delight that I was living with friends and working on my writing. She asked whether I needed money. When I said no, I could hear the relief in her voice. I claimed to be living in Will's parents' basement, a burden to no one.

They took two vacations that summer, to Tuscany and Puerto Vallarta. Will told Jay—and Jay told me—that they had reduced their budget, being unable to rent out the house on the internet with me in it. But they never brought up the issue of money, and I was not about to bring it up myself.

My first screenplay was very short, based on one of Mark's anecdotes. The prescribed format for movie scripts took up so much space that it was hard to remember from one screen to the next which scene I was writing. My dialogue seemed terrible, so I wrote as little of it as possible. In the end it read like a treatment for a silent movie, or a short story full of superfluous, space-hogging interruptions like "EXT. BEACH—DAY." My second screenplay was slightly longer and slightly better. I took exemplary care of Lionel.

Peter swung by L.A. in August on his way home from Singapore, staying at Jay's house for six days. I was over there all day, every day. He had been accepted by Harvard long before he admitted it to us, he was going, and we could not get enough of him.

He had jet lag and slept at odd hours, and Jay drifted into consciousness around eleven. But every morning around nine, after Jay's parents went to work, I drove from Will's house over to Jay's. His family's maid, Esme, let me in the front gate, and I snuck past the house and went skinny-dipping.

The pool was up the hill, in a corner of the lot, screened from the house by a row of cypresses. I could swim if my toes were touching the bottom of the pool. (That is, I could not swim.) When I got tired of splashing around, I would sit on a lounger and eat a pomegranate off one of the trees that lined the high stucco wall topped with razor wire that shielded the property from prying neighbors.

My aquatic forays were prompted by motives of the purest exhibitionism. It got me high to imagine disrobing in front of Peter. Little porn clips played in my head. It was highly unlikely, however, that he would see me, because I usually pretended to swim for all of two minutes before I got out to eat pomegranates with my clothes on, and he sometimes slept until noon. But I liked the adrenaline. He had hooked me on cheap thrills, and we both knew better than to expect time alone at Jay's place. When awake, Jay never took his eyes off Peter, and Peter—to avoid fostering delusions that we were alone—never came downstairs until he heard Jay.

I had not used the pool since middle school. The water stung my eyes. It was as chlorinated as the ocean was salty. I had never owned a swimsuit. Shorts and a T-shirt are better for playing in the ocean. It was rare to see feminine skin at Redondo Beach, where ethnic groups with strict notions of modesty prevailed and white girls bobbed in the water like seal people, hands on their surfboards, in full-body neoprene.

After the pool I would go in the French doors from the terrace to the kitchen to drink coffee from the big percolator. Jay would get up, Peter would follow, and the day would begin.

Esme was gone by then. Her shift was four hours, but she did her work in two or less. If she had taken time to socialize with all her employers, she would have had a ninety-six-hour week.

———

Indirectly, Jay's public shaming after the eurythmy debacle had taught him to dance. He had arrived in Málaga unable to go on as though he were blind. He had acquired a modicum of social ambition and realized how much more attractive he was when he stopped dancing. We had to beg him to show us even a little bit, and when he did, we were shocked at how good he was. His movements were minimized and subdued. A quick return to a neutral position followed every reluctant flourish. Stomps came only occasionally, punctuating restrained but accurate shuffling, a distant memory of the percussion jams of yesteryear. He gave the appearance of keeping intense emotion under tight control. Losing interest in flamenco had lent him the manly gravitas necessary for its performance. But he really had lost interest.

I commented, "It makes absolutely no difference why you're dancing so well. You should still show Loretta."

"No way," he said. "I'm pissed off at that bitch. She should have been making me do recitals. She taught me for seven years and never gave anyone a chance to tell me I looked like a dumb faggot. I should have been a bullfighter, not a dancer. That's what homosexuals do in Spain."

Disquieted, I said, "I thought she was your friend."

"She hung out with me for forty bucks an hour. She's no more my friend than my nanny was my mother."

Now shocked, I said, "I think Loretta is nice."

"She's all yours," he said graciously. "I'll give you her number."

"Oh, no, thanks," I said. I liked her, but I knew I was too shy ever to call her. She was too smart. She would immediately know why—that it was because Jay was dumping her.

"Spain has made a man of you," Peter observed. "In the negative sense."

"Nah, I don't think so," Jay said. "Because, face it, I would look so great in a bullfighting outfit. They call it 'suit of lights.' Imagine me poking a pink tablecloth with a wooden sword while some huge-ass bull's horns are zooming past my nipples. It's fucking perverted." He shuddered appreciatively.

"Bullfighters don't get to dance," Peter said. "They barely move."

"That's the key," he replied. "You stand there like a moron while this bull *impales* your ass. That's what makes it super gay. They die all the time. I would have gone to a bullfight, but I was too scared."

"You should just stay away from Spain. Keep a safe distance from all things Spanish."

"That's my plan."

Peter had altered his views on the subject of tragedy. "The latent fascism in postmodernity makes us incapable of it," he said by the pool, fully clothed and shading his eyes with *The New York Review of Books*. "Humanism is the lost prerequisite. Perhaps if we were capable of achieving humanity, I would never have fixated on tragedy as an ideal. But there's no return to the pre-fascist condition. All our dominant narratives are dystopian, but that's a dishonest term, a prevarication. Climate change, authoritarianism, and rape culture are not anti-utopias that would ring in utopia if they stopped. They dominate public discourse to slake our lust for humiliation, degradation, dehumanization, defilement, destruction [. . .]."

Jay said there were all kinds of kale-eating, goat-hugging, life-affirming anti-fascists around, if Peter would open his eyes.

"Where?" he said. "The internet is an openly fascist space. My condensed and purified avatar speaks for me, while I learn silence. Sure, I could move to a communal farm and strive for humanity, but it would be social self-erasure. The only narratives that break through to a shared reality are the ones that conform to a fascist aesthetic of dystopian entertainment, and that includes political and academic narratives [. . .]." He muttered something about Nick Land and the lure of the void.

"It's true," I said. "They show anti-fascists online all the time throwing rocks, but you never see them hugging goats."

"The goat-huggers online are, like, Christian housewives," Jay said. "They even hug chickens."

"I saw this video of a guy hugging a pelican," I said.

"So what's left to discourse now is the totality of the lack, the vacancy left by kitsch," Peter said. "Fascism pervades everything from the ground up."

"Aren't you being hard on yourself?" I asked. "All the media are fascist, and they fill your head with fascist thoughts, but are you sure you're infected? Because I don't think you're a fascist. It's like you're swimming in a septic tank, it's all around you, but you're actually still in one piece, inside your own skin, where there's no fascism."

"Everything that crosses the threshold of my eyes and ears is inside me," Peter said.

"That's not true!" I said. "If that were how it worked, I'd kill myself!"

"You're living proof," Jay said to me.

"But of what?" Peter asked.

"Proof you're not a fascist," I said.

"Ontological proof."

"Yeah. Whatever."

"One thing I love about you guys is that you're not very online," Peter said over dinner at a Mexican restaurant (Jay was paying), putting down his phone. He was the only one of us who kept his phone next to his plate during meals. "Most of the people I know are cyborgs training themselves to be bots, myself included."

"Online, I'd have to deal with strangers," I said. "I don't think strangers like me."

"That's what I mean," he said. "Everyone else is busy coming to terms with being a deceptive façade, the agony of reconciling algorithmic packaging with the living body, while you guys are still plotting your artistic debuts. You're like toddlers who think they're invisible when they close their eyes. Except that online, you're totally right."

Once he came inside to use the guest bathroom while I was pouring soda to take up to the pool on a tray. "I've loved seeing you here so much," he said. "It's been really wonderful." He reached out and petted the collar of my shirt.

"It's been nice for me, too," I said.

"Jay told me how you ended up at Will's house, by the way."

I gave him a pleading look. "Let's not talk about it. You probably know enough. Maybe more than I do."

"That's what paranoiacs always say."

I smiled. "Paranoia" was what he called all my non-delusions, from his love to the anger of the Hendersons.

He added, "If I knew three things about you, you would expect me to be able to derive the rest from inductive reasoning. So God knows what all you're not telling me."

I shook my head and said, "But I feel transparent. You can see through me like glass. I don't think there are more than three things to know about me anyway."

"You think I see what you see, and you don't see yourself. Maybe you never got to the mirror stage [. . .]. You're still using your eyes to see the world, instead of adopting the proper skewed perspective of an egomaniac. No wonder you're scared."

I stepped toward him and he hugged me. I said that if he carried the tray of sodas up to the pool, I would find and bring us something to eat.

"Your modest clothing looks theocratic to me now," Peter said as the three of us strolled past a row of fishermen on the Manhattan Beach pier, peering into their buckets and coolers to see the fish.

"Huh? What?" I said. "Theocratic?"

"I know you're hiding because it comes naturally to you, the way a squirrel hides by having fur. But in the booty-shorts-positive context of this pier, you look Opus Dei. Like a lay nun getting ready to stake out an abortion clinic. It's me. Brunei will do things to you. They don't show a lot of skin in Brunei. Skin is very political there."

"Bran's just modest," Jay said. "Plus she dresses like a dyke, not a religious fanatic."

"More like 'queer,' the kind that doesn't mind if their girl-friend has male genitalia."

"Isn't that being straight?" I asked, miffed.

"It's a question of whether genitalia make an artistic con-tribution," Peter said. "Gender, genre: same word. Sexuality is just the medium."

"I wouldn't mind having a girlfriend whose male genitalia made an artistic contribution," Jay said.

I would have laughed, but Peter had hurt my feelings. I brooded over how Yasira, with her skilled deployment of genre—making him go to her dad, an educated postmodern cosmopoli-tan, as if they were characters in a Regency romance—had gone and won the game before I knew there was a game to play.

I said, "Genre art isn't as good as the other kind."

"That's a relevant point," Peter said.

"I know!"

"Identities are pure kitsch. But not yours. There, the jury's still out. You're sui generis, maybe. Sometimes I think you're destined to do great things."

I asked him to be more specific. He said that's not how oracles work. He suggested that if I wanted to know about my future, I should ask Mark and Susan how many years I could stay at their house.

After he was gone, Jay and I had a long debate over whether Yasira actually existed. Peter had talked about her only in the vaguest terms. He definitely had more to say about her father, who shared his interest in literature.

For Jay, her nonexistence would prove a mastery of lying and trickery on Peter's part that greatly discredited him. I, for my part, thought she was a cliché, but I believed in her, because of the pictures. Privately I saw the question as a trivial hypothetical. Peter needed me to change and keep changing—clearly wanted me to, hoped I would—while her character was set in stone because he wanted it that way. Jay could confirm that he had said, "Marriage is commitment to a future without futurity." His fiancée should be static while he remained dynamic, like me. But that also made us too volatile to get close to each other. Intimacy might blow us apart, and our future would be shared at opposite ends of the universe.

Soon thereafter, while I was busy revising a terrible script in my new PJs (pink plaid), Doug called to tell me I was needed at home. "You are sorely missed right now," he said. "We're bringing in the harvest, and your grandfather has had a stroke."

"The harvest" could have meant a lot of things, and he was not my grandfather, but a stroke was a stroke, so I asked how bad it was.

"Real bad," Doug said. "He can't talk. He can't get up. He can't wipe his own ass."

"And I am sorely missed," I said.

"Right you are."

I knew that Grandpa Larry did not want strangers—that is, home health aides "from the government"—coming into his house. He was entitled to all the finest care, having served in Vietnam (or rather, in the U.S. Air Force on Long Island during the Vietnam War) and had promptly enrolled in Medicare when he turned sixty-five. He was the only Henderson with health insurance, and so far the only one who had needed it. The family doctor, a retired idealist who charged ten dollars per office visit, had just managed to finish giving Axel his childhood vaccinations before he died. I had never seen a doctor in my life, because my mother disbelieved in medicine.

"Couldn't you get Eric or Roger to do it?"

"Pa asked for you. There are things he wants to tell you. He wants to apologize."

"I thought you said he couldn't talk."

"I know my own father," Doug said firmly. "He's dying and he wants you here."

I said I would think about it.

Within an hour, I had gotten dressed, put some underwear and a toothbrush in my backpack, and driven to Bourdon Farms. My lean-to was in use for storage, but under the trash bags full of empty beer cans and the moldy saddlebags, everything was right where I had left it. My sleeping bag was still turned down from the last time I got out of it, with my sleeping T-shirt centered on my pillow.

Grandpa Larry, as Doug had said, was more or less immobile and helpless. He could wag his head, moan all the vowels, and gesture limply with his left hand. Doug tried to give him a drink of Ensure from a training cup while he shook his head. It dribbled down his beard.

The next time I came into the room, without Doug, he blinked at me ten or fifteen times. There were tears on his eyelashes and his nose was running. He made a grasping motion. I shook his hand and cleaned his nose with a wad of toilet paper while he moaned, "Ee-ee."

I thought he might mean "TV," so I tuned the receiver to the Jimmy Swaggart channel—of the things he liked to watch, the only one I could stand—where Grace Larson was singing a song called "The Promise." He shut his eyes and swallowed hard. He opened them wide and moaned a blue streak, all the vowels and then some, while his left hand pawed the covers like a croupier's rake.

He seemed to want something. There was a 7-Eleven cup half-full of melted ice on the bedside table. I sniffed it and was surprised to find it contained only H_2O.

"You have the DTs," I said to him. "Doug isn't giving you anything to drink. Am I right?" He hit his right hand with his left as if he were clapping.

The liquor in the house was always in plain view, a mixed crowd on the kitchen counter with dusty empties and undesirables on the floor beside the fridge. I found a nice bottle of bourbon still intact—the good stuff he had always denied to Doug and Axel, not by hiding it but simply by telling them it was his—and made him a stiff drink in a coffee cup, with fresh ice and the 7-Eleven straw.

He drank it up and instantly fell asleep. The room started to stink and I remembered what Doug had said about his ass.

I went outside to look for help. I expected everyone to be on the back lot somewhere, repotting or loading a truck or riding dirt bikes or whatever, but they were gone, and so were both trucks.

Axel and the latest Roger came home before Doug and Eric. It was eight p.m., after rush hour, but nobody mentioned being hungry, as if they had stopped off to have dinner on their way home from a delivery. Roger showed me how to roll Grandpa Larry over and get him into a new diaper, as though he had worked in a hospital at home in Gabon. He assured me that a woman has the strength to do it alone and left quickly, looking guilty.

I was too horrified to want to eat. The old man's condition had stricken me with mental collapse and surrender. After I cleaned him up, I sat by him again. Phrases from "The Promise" looped in my head. "Don't make this world your home . . . you'll surely be despised . . ." I thought about my mother. I felt her. Not as I had known her. With my senses I had known her as a slight blond woman, given to sudden motionlessness and staring, who liked to rest her nose on mine. What I felt was based on new knowledge, which Grandpa Larry was imparting to me, about how it feels to die.

Around eleven I texted Susan that I would be away overnight, explaining about Grandpa Larry. Mark called to ask if I was okay. He wanted to know details of the symptoms, as if he were a hobby practitioner of telemedicine. He seemed to think the old man was malingering. "You can't fool me, Bran," he said. "I can tell you're stressed out. Just say the word, and we'll pick you up. You don't need to do this. He's not even your grandfather!" Susan got on the line to remind me that I was very welcome in their home for as long as I wanted.

I said I would be back soon. Even as I said it, I could feel the spell taking hold. I had meant to say I'd be back in the morning, and suddenly I was telling them I would not stay away forever. It had a fairy-tale cast, like I might be gone for seven years.

———

They called every day at first, clearly worried. Twice in the first week, they knocked on the door to check on me personally, claiming to want to know whether I needed anything. Mark gestured meaningfully at their car, as if to say, Get in the car.

I feigned obliviousness. I had no needs. I was back in the environment I had sprung from, where needs were not encouraged. It would not be forever. Grandpa Larry would die, and then my life would go on.

But he hung on like a trouper. He was not one to let death get him down, at least not when regularly supplied with food and liquor. His condition was eerily stable, neither deteriorating nor improving. Would he have recovered from the stroke without all the whiskey I was giving him? If there was an answer to that question, I did not want to know, because he wanted to eat and drink and I was willing to keep him happy for as long as he was bedridden. He seemed like he might die any day. He was as harmless as a baby, and quieter. He was suffering and needed help. I could not make myself get up and leave. Roger, the competent nurse, was gone (for the first time in memory, he had not been replaced) and Doug was enjoying his newfound power. I remembered how Grandpa Larry had quit smoking in his late sixties, about ten years before, on principle, because so much of the price was taxes. At the time Doug had disagreed with him about the reality of inflation, pointing to Moore's law and its effect on computer equipment, pornography, and sex work, concluding with the claim: "Girls now you can get for eight dollars, they used to be a hundred and forty. I don't care what the girl looks like or how young she is, eight dollars with a condom is the right price." The logic was off, but after the stroke he was eager to limit his father's daily ration to the five cigarettes that were the theoretical equivalent of a pack and a half ten years ago and the cup of Ensure that was the equivalent of beans and franks with bourbon last month. Grandpa Larry would have starved.

Doug and Axel proclaimed that they had put aside all doubts that I was family. Every time they went shopping, they brought back pears and my favorite oatmeal cookies. I hardly spoke to them, but I ate the snacks, standing out back among the plants, far from the vile sights and sounds of the sickroom.

Jay came to see me on a Sunday, and we sat on the porch for a while. He said not a word about the way I looked (dusty) or acted (taciturn). He knew it well enough. I had readapted. He wanted to be kind and distract me, so he told me about his new dance hobby, contact improvisation. The dancers gathered for a set period of time and invented dances to do with one another. They were allowed to touch. It was emotionally and physically risky, because people would sometimes run and leap at the wrong people, expecting to be caught, or try to touch people who disliked them. It gave him an intense adrenaline high. "It's like having a panic attack from stage fright," he said, "but without the pressure. You can react any way you want. It's like, your brain's not working, but you're not allowed to talk anyway, so who needs a brain? You should try it sometime, so you know what I'm talking about."

We discussed whether it was fascist. Being forbidden to talk seemed potentially fascist, but it was egalitarian for everyone except for the person collecting rent on the studio.

The theme of fascism inevitably led us to talk about Peter. The word itself was like asking permission, a prelude to foreplay, something to mention when we had Peter on our minds and wanted to go there.

I asked Jay whether he had told him where I was. "Of course not," he said. "He'd freak out."

Peter texted, wanting to know whether I was writing. He said he was sorry not to be in touch, because the new college was keeping him very busy. I said I was taking time off to learn more about myself, and without even asking what I meant, he said it was a good idea and signed off "to prepare a class." After that I stared at the phone. Was he already a teaching fellow? He had only been there a couple of weeks.

Grandpa Larry slept a lot. Every few days one of his friends came by to stand awkwardly in the doorway for ten minutes, tell him what was going on in the world of outlaw bikers, and wish him well. He had been disenfranchised, and their visits made him sad.

During the day I kept house and cared for him, and at night I took short walks, seldom leaving the property, thinking about all I had never lost, never having had it. In between, I sat with him and watched Jimmy Swaggart.

There were other preachers on the channel, but the highlights for him were reruns of the younger Jimmy. If he could have spoken, I would have asked whether he ever had a phase of attending revivals. I could imagine a big camp tent with a stage and a choir, pitched right there at Bourdon Farms in the 1960s, with rows of Triumphs and Indians lined up outside, and a cordon of vets ready to rough up the peacenik Jesus freaks (Matthew 10:34, "I came not to send peace, but a sword"). However, even if he could have spoken, he would never have given me a straight answer, so it was six of one, half a dozen of the other. Nothing mattered. I waited for the channel to replay the Grace Larson song.

This went on for two months. Text exchanges with Peter and Jay were monosyllabic. Conversations with the Hendersons over meals in front of the TV likewise. Cook, clean, roll, wipe, tidy up, light cigarettes, change the channel, sing along with Grace, endure, vegetate—an emotional Arctic expedition. I felt increasingly proud of my survival, and wondered what other tough situations I might be adequate to. Previously, I had not considered my potential to achieve financial independence by hiring on with an Alaskan fishing boat or placer gold mine. Now, as I lay brooding myself to sleep nights, I felt capable of anything. I could have faced a prison sentence without trepidation, or joined the Islamic State.

In short, I no longer cared what happened to me. Nothing significant could happen to me, because things that mattered— good things, bad things—happened to me with Peter, and he was not there. In related news, I was the happiest I had ever been at Bourdon Farms, because I knew him.

CHAPTER EIGHT

O n the first Saturday in November, around eight o'clock in the morning, I heard a forceful knocking at the front door, as though the FBI had finally come for the Hendersons. I turned off the vacuum cleaner and went to answer it. It was Peter in a tweed overcoat. The look on his face veered from smiling into perturbation. He seized my right hand, palm up, and began stroking it with his fingertips. It was a strange, shy, shocked way of touching me, but effective. It was like a scale model of physical intimacy, reduced to a conceivable size. "It's good to see you," he said. "I just got off the plane. I hope your car still runs, because I told the taxi driver to leave. Let's go."

"Grandpa Larry—" I said.

"We can talk about him," he said. "But not here."

"He's sick."

"He has family."

"How did you know where I am?"

"Jay told me, last Monday. As if he'd been trying to protect me. Fucking jerk."

I agreed to fetch my keys, but some instinct told me to pack for the last time. I hesitated in front of my cardboard box of clothes for a moment, finally selecting some intact underwear and a clean shirt. The only valuables not already in my pockets were the three fantasy novels, so I put them in my backpack. Grandpa Larry was sleeping. I could text Doug (he had passed out in a lawn chair by the ashes of his party bonfire, and Axel was upstairs with a woman) when I was safely away and hard to find.

I ran to my car. Peter was waiting beside it, holding the passenger-side door handle, blandly admiring the sky. He showed no interest in signs of life from the house—there was shouting—and neither did I. Nothing trumped Peter, *ni dieu ni maître*.

Regularly referring to his phone, he steered us to a hotel in downtown L.A. that had its own underground parking garage. He directed me all the way down the ramp and into my spot.

In the elevator up to the lobby we stood so close to each other that I could feel the stiff edges of his coat poking into my skin. It felt sensitized somehow, as if I were coated with Tiger Balm.

The hotel was unlike any building I had ever been inside before. It had a high polygonal atrium and planters everywhere. The architecture of everything but the doorways used oblique angles, as if it had been designed by an anthroposophist. All the vertical surfaces were exposed aggregate or dark wood, with touches of brass and smoked mirrors. There were dozens of overstuffed brown leather armchairs scattered across a tiered landscape of glistering taupe carpet. It was a place that had once been luxurious but had lost the race for the rich customers to modern glass and marble, and Peter said he could put it on a special American Express card that his parents had given him for emergencies. He picked out a group of chairs in a distant corner of the lobby, with a view out the panoramic windows of a plaza lined with food trucks and dotted with people eating. We took turns going to the bathroom. Then I waited with our luggage while he checked us in. He kept his coat on, because the lobby was freezing cold.

Of course our room was not ready. He said, "We can go out and maybe find some breakfast."

He parked our stuff at reception, and we went down to the plaza and wandered around. Nothing looked edible to us. We kept touching each other with our fingertips. I felt weightless and somehow taller, as if we were both floating. We held each other's hands for a minute, but it was hard to get around that way, because it somehow made us incline our upper bodies toward each other, so we stopped. We circled the plaza at least twice, not crossing any streets.

Finally, he gave up and said we could get room service if we got hungry, or come back to the plaza later. "I promise we won't starve," he said.

We rode the elevator back upstairs to the lobby and waited for another ten minutes, and then finally they gave him our card key.

He insisted on carrying my backpack while he pulled his suitcase to the room. It was on the fifth floor, one of many narrow doors facing a long indoor balcony that ran around the atrium, with a view across the bed of mountains obscured by a hazy late-fall day, an atmosphere tinged with smoke.

Somewhere far off, something was burning. But the air in the room was clear, fresh, and cool. The moment we entered the room, it pushed us apart.

I stood at the window and said, "If I'd known you were getting a place this nice, I would have said let's go to the desert."

"I never thought about the part where we leave the room." He sat down on the bed, with pillows piled up behind him, and elucidated, "I'm here to deprogram you. Take your shoes off and get over here."

I stepped forward and stood at the edge of the bed. I was not afraid. But not because I was tough, or indifferent to my fate. If anything, I had become something of a complete and total wreck in my months at Grandpa Larry's bedside. I would not have lasted five minutes on a fishing boat or in prison. In my nervousness I was feeling the first glimmerings of self-esteem. I knew what it was like to fear that I was about to perform a har-rowingly unpleasant act, and this was not that. This was some-thing supremely good for me, and of no import to anyone else but Peter. I had to stay still, to give the feeling time to expand.

"Shoes off," he said. "You want me to take them off?"

"I can take off my own shoes," I said. I sat down on the bed and he leaned forward and put his arms around me. I elbowed him in the ribs, softly, so I could take off my shoes. I turned and lay down.

We lay face-to-face, not moving, breathing together, gently hugging each other. We were free to do whatever we wanted, and we did just about nothing. He kissed my eyebrows and said, "Oh, Bran. You're so sweet, and you've been through so much."

I cried, surrendering to my new situation. It was not the old situation. He had uprooted me, permanently, and I was resting on my way to being repotted.

If I had known more love in my life, I could never have been that happy. If he had been sexually experienced (or unscrupu-lous, or undignified), he could have turned our happiness into thrashing, a state of exception to be washed off and forgotten, and I would have spent the night there and gone home to Bourdon Farms. But he had not thought past love itself, and in all my mental explorations I had never thought of this: that I could be so happy.

After a while, it got to be time for us to shift positions, and he pushed himself upright and said, "Don't be mad, but I brought work with me. I have to read about two hundred pages and put together a bibliography by tomorrow night. My professor is a slave driver." He pulled five or six books out of his suitcase and stacked them among the pillows. He picked up the one called *Pouvoirs de l'horreur: Essai sur l'abjection* and began to read, stopping almost instantly to ask whether I was thirsty.

I was horrendously thirsty. I jumped up and drank four glasses of water in the bathroom. I brought him a glass of his own and lay down again at his side, relaxing into a blissful state that gave way to an endless vision of curly wires connecting sparkling golden mirrors—the universe as an Olafur Eliasson light fixture—as I fell asleep.

Waking up, I rolled over and found myself facing him. He said he was famished. His laptop was open to a document full of book titles and page numbers, but there was a long wrinkle down the side of his face, as though he had recently been sleeping on it.

We went downstairs. It was dark out and the food trucks had moved on, so we ate in the hotel restaurant, a square space demarcated from the lobby by a frosted glass partition, with frosted windows and horseshoe-shaped booths that were almost separées, velvet curtains above their high wooden walls. Each table had a tea light burning in a little purple glass. There were only four other customers. He ordered rack of lamb. I ordered fettucine alla carbonara. Over our house salads, we toasted his parents with tap water for buying us dinner. For dessert we split a tiramisù, because I had never heard of it. After dinner I took a bath while he worked. After some discussion, around three o'clock in the morning, we drove to the desert.

First I checked the oil and coolant and talked to my car—he laughed at me—because you have to talk to vehicles. (I had thought it was universal, but I guess people with reliable cars get out of the habit.) The traffic was light and the air was orange. With every row of hills, the sky darkened and gained stars. Then dawn came, fading them all. We stopped at a wayside to breathe the cold, transparent air.

For him, it was a new experience. In his year at UCLA, he had not gone to the desert once.

He said the transparency unnerved him. Here a tree, there a tree, but all of them yuccas, narrow and twisting, widely spaced, so that through this forest, distant hills were visible, as if there were no forest. He said he had never seen a forest like that. We had pancakes at a truck stop in Yucca Valley at his parents' expense and drove into Joshua Tree National Park just before seven thirty. The gates stood open with no one around, except for a shy stray dog or coyote.

The rock piles were vivid orange in the morning light. We trundled over rough asphalt to the third or fourth climbable-looking pile, parked nearby, and climbed it. It was wonderful to place our hands cautiously on its sandpapery solidity. The warm beauty of the rocks was radiantly clean. The birds warbled and ricocheted. The multicolored sky unfurled from blue into yellow. We stood side by side on top of the highest rock, facing the low, bright sun.

Below us, cars and RVs crowded the uneven road. A big

family was jockeying around the base of our rock pile, shouting at one another about the best way up. I had never felt so free, so safe, or so close to anyone.

It was literally true. I had never been so free. I had never been so safe. I had never been so close to anyone.

We drove to a picnic area that had nothing much to see—a couple of rock outcroppings, a crow, a lizard—and got out of the car again. He regretted aloud his failure to spend time in the desert, saying that he should have known that his soul would expand if his eyes saw nothing near and familiar; that he must reread Bachelard's *Poetics of Space;* that he barely recognized me, de-contextualized as a limber, hazel-eyed animal springing from rock to rock; along with various statements I am pretty sure were incoherent. Nothing was suited for a "[. . .]". It was more like "[.] [?] [!]."

We rode around some more, climbed another rock pile, walked a nature trail, and started back around noon, stopping at a food truck for tacos. I was sleepy, so he drove.

We had not checked out of the hotel or even packed our things, so his parents had already paid for an extra night. He worked a little more, reading and typing, while I rested beside him.

He said he would not leave town until he knew I was either at Jay's house or back with Mark and Susan. He would get a taxi to the airport from my destination.

"So where do you want to go?" he asked.

"Harvard," I said. "I can live in your room."

"Yasira would not be down with that," he said.

Feeling truly sad for the first time in months, I frowned—an untethered astronaut regarding her space capsule as it receded, realizing how little her feelings mattered anywhere outside her head.

"I can't help loving you," he said. "My affection for Yasira is manageable. I don't want to love my wife come hell or high water. That would be an open invitation to hell and high water, to inundate my life. I'd rather have you as the Lady of the Lake. I'll be Merlin. We'll always have the crystal cave." His eyes rested calmly on mine. He smiled.

"You absolutely cannot stop fucking with me, can you," I said.

He looked down, as if he were embarrassed.

"But it's okay," I said. "I would rather be fucked with by you than fucked by any man in the universe!" Then we really kissed. Like, serious, hard-core kissing. His hands even got partway into my pants. We rolled around on the bed.

We returned to silent mutual contemplation. He studied me in his scholarly way, tallying hairs and pigments, and I let myself be happy again.

I drove him to the airport, instead of letting him get a cab, because it gave us more time together and saved explaining things to Mark and Susan. It was hard to imagine how he and I would justify his parting from me on their doorstep on a Sunday night when they had thought I was with Grandpa Larry. My concern about this issue was enough to convince him that I truly intended to go to their house.

I still had their spare key, but I rang the doorbell, and they welcomed me like the prodigal son.

———

"Larry Henderson," Mark said. "Where do I begin. When Doug was about fifteen, there was an incident connected with the high school. This was while I was in law school at USC. There was a party down at the beach that got out of hand, with this girl on speed and LSD giving oral to this kid under a blanket in front of everybody. She didn't know where she was, or who she was with. She wasn't involved with Doug or anything, but he liked her and thought it was unfair and I guess it spoiled the party for him, because he went home and told his dad about it. People didn't have phones yet. Thank God this was before people had video cameras on their phones. I wouldn't want to be young now. So Larry Henderson gets it into his head that a good girl has been raped, and gets together a posse to terrorize the perpetrator. I should mention that this kid was Black. Actually mixed-race, from someplace in the Midwest, and falling-down drunk. So anyway, first Doug leaves the beach party on his motorcycle, and an hour later there are outlaw bikers there, looking for this kid. Of course they found him. He had nowhere to run, so he ran in the ocean and fucking drowned. Died in two feet of water because he was too drunk to stand up! Nobody laid a hand on him. He went in on his own, like it was suicide in self-defense. Larry never left Bourdon Farms that night. That image still bothers me. Larry Henderson drinking a nightcap with his son on his front porch, and a Black kid's body rolling back and forth on the sand because his classmates are afraid to fish him out."

"What a bunch of pussies," I said. "I mean, unless the bikers were swinging chains, I would have charged every person on that beach with manslaughter. Nobody should die because his friends are pussies!"

He laughed nervously and said that was not the reaction he was expecting, but that the kids were in fact such obligate pussies that they all refused to give statements to the police.

"You can't let people like Grandpa Larry control you," I said. "That's how you turn into Doug."

He remarked that I seemed to have learned some gumption somewhere. "You seem stronger," he said.

Susan bought me three pairs of leggings from an online yoga outfitter. At first I said no, no, no. But she refused to return them. She insisted that they were what young women wore.

I tried them on. They were obscene and wasteful—I had never worn pants that got dirty so fast—but no less comfortable than baggy jeans.

Her next step in immodest fashion behavioral therapy was to put me in bras that fit, from the lingerie department of an old-fashioned department store. When I had found one, she handed me a T-shirt she had picked out. It looked as tiny as one of her socks, but it fit over my upper body with room to spare.

Then she pushed me in front of the three-way mirror by the entrance to the dressing rooms with her hand in the small of my back, and said, "Now look at yourself. Look. Who's that? That's you. That's Bran." She was right to say it, because I was literally thinking, *Who the fuck is that?* Her method was very Milton Erickson. "You look like a million dollars," she added. "I would kill to be your age, but I never looked like that. You look perfect."

"My hands," I said, holding them up like paws, with my fingertips down. I still had calluses on the tops of my knuckles.

"They have hand models for that," she said. "Nobody's hands are all that great. You're a knockout. You're one of the beautiful people who can dress up by taking things off. You know who you look like? Natalie Portman! Now stand up straight and pull your shoulders down."

I wondered how Mark was going to be able to keep his mouth shut and his hands to himself when he saw me. He had always been polite to Fifi, no matter how she dressed or made herself up, but some pitiful learned instinct told me he would treat me differently.

He took in my tits and ass at a glance, smiled, and ignored them from thenceforth. He treated my body like an A on a test, not a personal challenge. He was a decent man.

It was he who taught me to walk like a girl. Susan was unable to deduce exactly how it was done, but he had a theory drawn from long years of furtive glancing at asses. "Keep your knees close together," he said. "Walk as if there's a rubber band connecting your knees." I tried it, and it worked. "Excellent!" he said. "Now, that's enough femininity. More than that would be déclassé."

"He's right," she said. "You're way too tall for miniskirts."

"Feminine good, streetwalker bad," he said. "We're striving for a feminine look that commands respect."

"Is that even possible?" I asked.

They both laughed, and she said, "You're so funny."

Several days later, during dinner, they instigated a conversation. They felt I was ready for the workforce. A mere high school graduate's options were indeed limited—similar to those of a convicted felon—but there were non-nightmarish positions available. Specifically, they imagined me behind the counter of an upscale chain coffee shop. My former look would have condemned me to a uniformed fast-food role, probably behind the front lines, in the bowels of the kitchen. Cleaned up, in skin-tight clothes, I looked ready to accept a one-dollar tip for making change.

I volunteered that I could also do yard work. The idea had come to me right before I had come to them, and I had put it out of my mind, but it was still valid. "Aren't coffee shops where students work?" I said. "Yard work probably pays better."

"You'd be depriving an undocumented immigrant of a job," Mark said. "With a corporate employer, you won't have to waste time badgering customers to pay their bills. Being self-employed is a boatload of paperwork, if you do it legally."

I had not considered doing it legally. The conscious impetus came from habit, but I also lacked photo ID and saw no reason to incriminate myself by pointing it out. I said cautiously, not wanting to tip my hand, "I'm not totally sure I can prove I'm a citizen."

He gave me a funny look. "What's the big deal?" he said. "I can notarize anything you want. We'll get you a duplicate birth certificate, and with that and your driver's license, you can get a passport and be a free woman. You could go to Europe."

In other words, they had no idea that I drove illegally and had enrolled in school on the strength of affidavits. I said, "Sure!"

They also had ideas about where I could live. Given my dearth of personal property, I was, in their view, a born house sitter. People with elderly dogs or finicky cats might hesitate to rent out their homes to vacationers. Many holiday destinations imposed restrictions and quarantines on pets. Some pets were too large to fit in bags, or too frisky to pass for service animals. As a result, there was regular demand, among Susan's acquaintances from the hospital, for people to sleep in guest rooms and care for dogs and cats for two to three weeks at a stretch.

"We don't want you feeling like you're a burden on us," she said. "You're always welcome here, *always,* but obviously none of us want this arrangement to be permanent. You need a springboard to independence, and a few house-sitting gigs would buy us all some time. I can't figure out what you should do next. Probably college, but where? And where do you live, and how do you pay for it? Though it wouldn't start until next fall anyway."

I nodded wisely, because her thinking was impeccable. Also, I liked the way she and Mark treated me as an equal, never suggesting I hire on at Walmart or an Amazon warehouse. They wanted me upwardly mobile or not at all.

I talked to Jay on the phone. He claimed that their aversion to tall streetwalkers was transphobic. "They didn't say streetwalkers are bad," I protested. "Just that I shouldn't dress like one."

He said, "Right."

"I'd be appropriating sex-worker culture."

"Like whores don't wear yoga pants! That's what I meant by transphobic. If I wanted to put on drag, I'd have to wear a skirt to hide my dick, but you can wear yoga pants. They're transphobic."

I could see his logic, but not really, and said, "How do you know your dick is such a big distraction to everybody if you never wear yoga pants?" After a pause, I added, "Please don't wear yoga pants."

———

Doug called to tell me I had killed Grandpa Larry. When I left, he had taken less than a week to go into a decline, hallucinating and refusing to take liquids. A hospice nurse had come at the end to give him morphine. "Excellent morphine," he added. He had died of a second massive stroke, provoked by the stress of my departure. Among his last words were bitter accusations, directed against me.

I said, "That can't be true. He couldn't talk."

"He could say 'Bran.' That's all he said. Calling out to you, and you weren't there. What did you do to him?"

Then he wanted to know if I had seen Grandpa Larry's DD 214 (discharge from the Air Force) anywhere, because he needed it to get him a slot at the L.A. National Cemetery. I said I had no idea where it might be. He mocked me, putting on a high, girly voice to say, *"I am not my grandfather's keeper,"* as if I had abdicated all responsibility for a dependent placed in my care. "I simply don't know why the fucker kept you in his will," he concluded.

That was another lie—there was surely no will; there were no official cash assets and no real property, just a lot of plants and a house full of silverfish—but I entertained it long enough to agree to attend the funeral. I definitely needed money, and I was definitely owed it. After approximately one minute, it was again obvious to me that Doug had lied. But I also thought the funeral would place a fitting caesura in my life. It could become the last time I saw Doug and Axel.

———

Susan, Mark, Will, Jay, Henry, and Peter all told me not to go. Fifi texted me that I should take advantage of the event to sneak back to Bourdon Farms and burn it down. I was not in touch with her—she got all her news from Jay—but she was never at a loss for strong opinions about my life. She had character.

The funeral was scheduled for two p.m. on the Monday before Thanksgiving. I had lunch with Jay (to my relief, he was not wearing yoga pants) because the cemetery was so close to UCLA. I wore a black cotton dress borrowed from Susan. I could wear her shoes, if they were sandals or open-toe. They were only about half a size too small. The dress was too big, which was fine with me. I wanted to look generic.

Eric and Roger—new ones I had never met—told me I looked nice. Axel and Doug were taken aback in exactly the way I had planned. The bikers emitted wolf whistles. Even their way of watching me was reminiscent of wolves. The preacher talked about Lawrence Henderson's heroic courage under enemy fire, as if he had been a decorated combat veteran. Airmen in full dress uniform folded the American flag from the coffin into a little triangle and presented it to Doug. The honor guard of middle-aged former warriors teared up, as though they felt bad about serving in the nineties, when America was at peace. After they fired off their salutes, the wolves started to circle. I walked and then ran back to my car. Running in heels is easier than walking in them. Running on tiptoe is natural.

Mark escorted me to the beachfront coffee shop where he liked to go on Saturdays and introduced me to the manager, who immediately welcomed me to the corporate family. I filled out a fictitious application a day later, on the clock. I was playing a childish role, but it was nice not to have to answer questions about what motivated me to sell coffee. The manager could have asked for proof of my legal right to work in the U.S., but he skipped nearly all the formalities, as though he owed Mark a favor. Mark was a public defender, after all, so maybe he did.

The other workers were college students and found it strange that I was not. Almost immediately, they began to evaporate home for the holidays, and I could have all the shifts I wanted.

My tips were redolent of holiday generosity and open flirtation. Unbeknownst to me and Susan—through our shared ignorance of the finer points of college culture—I had adopted the "basic bitch" look, the single most approachable genre of woman known to Californians. But none of the customers were wolves, and they could not have seized me if they tried. I was secure behind a counter piled high with merchandise.

I picked up double shifts on Christmas Eve, Christmas Day, New Year's Eve, and New Year's, sometimes getting a five-dollar tip on a five-dollar drink. Grandma Tessa and Grandpa Lamont were disappointed that I had not come to Pasadena for Christmas, but only until I put a price on it. Then they were happy for me.

After all those years in the nursery, it was hard for me as apply the term *work* to the act of placing a muffin in a paper bag with tongs. In terms of horsepower, my workload made my tips seem pretty unfair to people who worked on oil rigs or cleaning hospitals, and I said as much to Mark.

He made a speech to clear things up. "That's America," he

said. "Workers here wouldn't be called workers by Karl Marx. He'd call them *'Lumpenproletariat,'* the class below workers, with no class consciousness and no net worth, dressed in rags. Income in this country is a U-shaped curve. There are fewer people making eighty thousand dollars a year than making sixty or a hundred! A family can live on less than a hundred, but it's not easy."

The *Lumpen* description sounded just like my old job, but even my winter holiday pay-plus-tips rate at the coffee shop would have annualized to less than forty thousand dollars. Like any white-collar worker, I was being compensated for sacrificing life, not labor; the job consumed nothing but my time and a mess of carbon, like a traffic jam. But I had thought it was going to make me middle-class, as do-nothing jobs were supposed to do. I said, "Oh."

I got to see my high school friends over Christmas vacation, but not for long. Will had his first girlfriend. She was in Milwaukee, but nevertheless she kept him occupied. He hunched over his phone or held it tightly to his ear, sometimes in his car in the driveway for privacy. When the literary-magazine staff met up at a café, he left us to be with her. We could see him outside on the sidewalk, pacing up and down, being with her. The third time we all arranged to go out, he stayed home.

Henry and Fifi were back together. Neither of them told me the details, but Henry told Jay, who told me before he took off to Colorado with his parents to ski. According to Jay, Henry had hooked up with numerous skinny rich girls at Yale. It was something he had always wanted to try, and what better place than Yale? There were ethereal cosmopolitan actors in the drama department there, and dancers who were practically gymnasts. But it turned out they were working in a different genre. The coldhearted hookups made him sad. Meanwhile, Fifi persisted in her exclusive loyalty to him and her steely determination to become an orthodontist and be "rolling in it" for his sake. The current plan was for her to transfer to a school that was closer to Yale, probably UConn Storrs. They planned to rent their own apartment.

We sat together for hours, on four occasions, trading stories about college classes, professors, and TV shows—twice without Jay—but afterward it was always Jay who outlined the events of their lives to me, as if they were his cousins who lived in another state.

Will, Henry, and Fifi were not quite friends with me anymore. Maybe, barely. Not really. We were not going through things together. They still mattered to me, and I wanted them to be content, and for us to part after each meeting by hugging and drawing back, frowning slightly, as if we were each other's worried parents. But instead they were casual and festive. Will was a biologist in love. Fifi was an adult with a strategic life plan. Henry was a grown man who could turn sleazy hookups into a cautionary tale and be forgiven. And who was I? A clinically infatuated basic bitch.

They never asked to hear my story. Were they waiting for me to tell it on my own? I wish I knew. Henry told me I looked "very different." Fifi agreed, but she sized up my ass in a way that was not approving. I wanted her encouragement, but it would have been a bit awkward to sit down with her as if she were my boss and draft annual goals, so I gave up instantly.

When I finally drove to Pasadena to see Grandma Tessa and Grandpa Lamont, I wore Mark's castoffs again. My sexy look was not an option. They found me extraordinarily well groomed and prosperous.

Peter called to see how my screenplay was coming along. "I'm working at a coffee shop for tips," I said. "Mark called me the *Lumpenproletariat.*"

"You can tell Mark they've been a revolutionary class since Fanon," he said. Then he described how Jay's dancing had inspired him to write on the Suprematism of Kazimir Malevich. "An anti-aesthetic movement," he said. "Against sensation, in favor of the primacy of emotion. Entirely abstract art. Art for the blind. A Suprematist painting can be described as a set of coordinates."

"What's that got to do with emotion?"

"Nothing," he said. "If it made any sense, it would hardly be fertile ground for interrogation. I try to stay away from things that make sense. I hope you're not tempted to get mixed up with them."

"Oh, no, never," I said, nodding invisibly.

CHAPTER NINE

My first house-sitting job was for almost the entire month of January, in a place in Palos Verdes, up on the mountain, with a view of the ocean from the second floor. Outside the high wooden fence around the yard was a park full of brush and steep arroyos swarming with wildlife. The place was so pretty, and my role there so "normal"—so traditionally feminine and upper-middle-class—that it made even watching sunsets from my bedroom window seem like a celebration of social rebirth. I was like the gap-toothed girl in the Milton Erickson book, ready to embark on a future without a future. The commute to the coffee shop was longer, and business got slower after the Christmas rush, but the money held steady, and I was content. My high school friends texted me memes. Peter alternated vestigial anecdotes ("lol lost in the stacks") with confusing prompts ("ICYMI [link to a discussion of Cormac McCarthy in *Locus*] sf v. post-apocalypse") as if he had me mixed up with someone else. But it was me he wrote to, as if I were everyone, and that was good enough for me. Every night I got a video call from my ersatz parents, checking in and signing off with a wave of Lionel's paw.

The pets that necessitated my house-sitting were twin female sheep, Marge and Sideshow Bobbie. Their function was to trim the lawn and all the bushes up to a height of four feet while looking clean and white. They were loud and shat everywhere and the situation under their tails was unsettling. Every "baa" sounded like Axel's most playful burp, channeled through a megaphone. The neighbor's Shiba Inu ran unceasingly up and down the fence line, barking in outrage at their presence. I wondered whether they were legal, or in blatant defiance, or grandfathered. But it was not my problem. I fed them, watered them, and inspected them for wounds so that I could text my landlords that they were in good health. For the first time in my life, I was a tenant, in a purely commercial relationship with my hosts, rather than (for better or worse) a guest.

Twice a week, I let the Polish maid inside to tidy up. She had no keys of her own. After her first visit, when she dealt with fingerprints—transparent ones, as from hair product or croissants—there was not much for her to do. I kept things clean so she could relax with a feather duster, blasting urban contemporary radio on the quadraphonic system with woofers in the conversation pit.

A laconic Mexican groundskeeper came by on alternate days to rake soggy sheep shit off the lawn (the embedded irrigation system kept the yard damp), mow it, and muck out the shed.

After four weeks, my patrons returned from Cabo, tanned and rested. I beamed, thanked them, said, "See you next year, maybe!" and moved back to Mark and Susan's guest room.

That evening, Susan acted as though she needed to share a confidence, making me a cappuccino and sitting me down at the kitchen table. She informed me that she and Mark were having "marital troubles." She said he had been "distant." Then she said nothing, as though being purposely sparse and vague because she hoped I might volunteer relevant evidence.

It was hard for me to imagine what marital trouble in their world looked like. I mean, if he went to bed one night without kissing her and telling her he loved her, would it be the first time ever, the end of an era? They had always seemed so flawlessly affectionate to me, a utopian vision of a happy couple. Had they not been having sex? Did happy couples who had been married for twenty-five years have sex once a week, or once a month? It was an inopportune moment for me to wonder aloud. I surfaced to say, "I'm sorry," more appropriately than I knew.

She asked whether I was making any progress in finding my own place.

Suddenly it was plain that she thought I was causing her conflict with Mark, or at least that she willing to sacrifice me in the interest of finding out whether I might not be the cause of her conflict with Mark.

I said, "Not yet, but I'll keep trying!"

I had not tried. To my mind, she had insinuated—basically promised—that with her connections in the rich doctor community, she could get me cushy livestock-sitting jobs from here to kingdom come. I was still pushing the rope of the future in six-week stretches. Kingdom come, as I understood it, would take place whenever life performed its next radical deviation. I was in no rush to get there.

I decided that her feelings were like one of those rogue waves near the Cape of Good Hope, when a combination of random sloshing from all directions piles up into a pyramid a hundred feet high and swamps a tanker. Her marriage was already as long as the ocean is wide, so there had to be unpredictable quantum effects, unless psychology was involved after all, and seeing me around had made her wish she were nineteen again and she projected those feelings onto Mark. Or he called my name in his sleep and wanted sex in the morning before he brushed his teeth? I had no idea, but I felt pressure to leave their house.

In February my boss got a tip that ICE might be coming through the strip mall where our coffee shop was located. This was no big surprise. The strip mall included a building supply store with a mini-lumberyard. The coffee shop had been built out next to the intersection, separate from the other stores, and had its own little walled parking lot, so that migrants looking for day labor liked to sit on our wall every morning, starting at five. We never asked them to leave, partly because we were nice, and partly because the builders and renovators who hired them nearly always bought coffees, and sometimes boxes of coffees for entire crews. My boss wondered aloud whether I might be willing to come up with a photo ID plus birth certificate or Social Security card for his files. I said I would bring them in when I had them all, but that was not good enough. He needed to be able to show ICE that he had carded me before I started. Otherwise he could get in trouble. He wanted them the very next day.

I said there was literally no way, so he fired me. He had no choice. I could stay for a complimentary coffee and baked good, if I took off my name badge. Otherwise, there was a danger ICE would take me for an employee, fine him big money, and haul me away to migrant jail.

"I grew up at Bourdon Farms," I said. "I'm so American it hurts."

"No American is more American than others," he corrected me. "We are very equal as citizens. But you must be able to prove it."

"I'm sorry," I said. "I didn't mean to imply that being American is a good thing. It isn't always, really."

He corrected me again. He had grown up a Berber in Algeria and had lived there until he was fifty-two. All the values were still fresh in his mind. Freedom, opportunity, all the other privileges from which I failed to profit. My business model was a beggar's tin cup, plus leggings.

I drove back to Mark and Susan's house and took Lionel out for a walk around the block, a big square. Halfway through it, I heard Harleys coming about a quarter mile off ("loud pipes save lives") and started looking around for a place to hide. But I was afraid to take Lionel into strangers' carports, or through their side yards onto their back lawns. It would have laid me open to accusations.

In the end I ran back, because I thought I had time to get in the front door. But the bikers had already delegated someone to block my way.

The delegated biker—a familiar and wolfish young face known to me as Loki—folded his arms, stood with his legs far apart, and said, "Branny Thomas, we don't know what you did to Larry, RIP, but we're commanding you to take it back and let his soul rest. You come around when he's dying, cast a spell on his mind, make him die saying your name, you fucking witch. If you was related by blood, you'd have had a right to be in there, you could take his property, take his soul—we don't care, do we—am I right? We're fair people, with the laws of inheritance, but that's not how we roll, is it, when you ain't ever been nothing to nobody over to Bourdon Farms. Doug and them don't know who the fuck you are. But we know your mother worshipped Satan, am I right? That's all we need, 'cause we ain't fucking stupid. You're a piece of shit and a thieving witch, Branny whoever-the-fuck you are, and you're going down!"

There was general assent in the crowd of five bikers, and Lionel said, "Woof!"

I said nothing. I was fighting not to close my eyes, fall down, and pee.

A subordinate biker dismounted from his bike. He stepped forward to unfurl something that was inconspicuous in his hand but large when extended to full size—a dead seagull—and threw it at my legs. Lionel and I cowered. Another biker shouted, "Come on, take her out!" but Loki shook his head. As he left, he walked so close to me that he stepped on a seagull wing. The bikes revved and growled and they all rode away.

I locked myself and Lionel in the house, and called Mark. That call went to voice mail, so I tried Susan, who also was only available as voice mail. I texted them both, but got no answer. I wanted one of them to tell me whether I should call the police.

The question was moot, since a neighboring retiree had taken that step the second the bikers showed up. No one filmed them. (It was lunchtime, and everyone else in the neighborhood under age sixty-eight was at work or school.) Ten minutes later I was shivering outside, watching a detective take measurements of the seagull while two uniformed cops looked for boot prints in the gutter.

I denied over and over that I had any idea who those guys might be. Supposedly, I had never seen them before in my life. Hauntingly, I remembered my ungenerous critique of the kids on the beach who saw their friend drown. Then I remembered how smart it is never to say anything to cops—not one word—so I shut up, professing exhaustion.

They sympathized. The detective said he would be back to talk to Mark, whom he rated a likely target for threats from groups hostile to law enforcement.

The prospect of the coming evening frightened me—to sit with Susan and Mark for hours while they drank red wine and waffled, trying to find a tactful way to tell me to move out on the day I lost my job.

Instead of making myself something to eat, I put all my stuff in my car. In two and a half months of work, I had saved almost fourteen hundred dollars in small bills. For a couple of nights, I could afford a motel in Riverside. I was in that rare and special state of mind when a person feels safest on Hells Angels turf. Grandpa Larry and his friends were allied with their archenemies, the Bandidos.

I drove east for an hour, checked into a Motel 6 by the freeway, pulled the curtains, turned on all the lights, and arranged myself on the bedspread with my books.

Now I had four instead of three: *The Once and Future King, The Crystal Cave, The High King,* and *Minima Moralia* by Theodor W. Adorno, a gift from Peter.

"For Marcel Proust," I began, reading aloud.

Mark and Susan each called several times. I rejected the calls, eventually texting them that I was in hiding, lying low for their protection. Mark immediately called to insist that the whole thing could be cleared up if I came home and spoke with him openly. They were worried. I told him not to be worried. If my car were parked near his house, he could worry, but as it stood, he had no reason to worry.

He demanded to know where I was. I refused to divulge that information. He got pissed off. Then Susan got on the line. I was weakening—close to giving in—so I hung up on them and called Grandma Tessa. "Hey," I said. "How are you? How's Grandpa?" She was so wonderfully incurious about my exact doings and whereabouts, always happy to hear that I was alive and in good health. I assured her that I was feeling great, doing well, having fun, making money, you name it. My having a cell phone liberated her from the obligation to care where I was. All I needed to do was answer it, had she ever called.

I did not text Peter. I knew he was idealistic and inexperienced and would underestimate the conciliatory effects of sobering up. By this time tomorrow, the wolves would have an entirely new set of priorities. Their attention spans were vanishingly short. Unless someone in the group was genuinely obsessed with my legacy hunting or my wicked ways, they would soon forget me. There was no point in crying wolf unless things got undeniably hairy.

Contacting Jay was out of the question. Any information I gave him would spread to the others. Henry and Fifi would dissect me in a group chat and post my picture as a missing person.

I turned off my phone and read my new book. I had to read every sentence at least ten times, meditating over paragraphs like mantras, until their meaning suddenly appeared.

"There is no right life in the wrong one," for instance. That was how Adorno denied the possibility of human happiness in functionalistic housing projects with crappy furniture. I had never read a book so rigorous and mundane—the parts I understood, at least, meaning maybe one sentence in twenty.

I had bathed so long in the unconditional love of Mark and Susan that it did not immediately occur to me that they might regard my behavior as erratic. When it finally did, that night around eleven, I felt a great sympathy. They had been spoiled by having a son they raised themselves. They never knew what he would do next, but they had contrived to narrow his horizons. Where Will would go to grad school, what public-spirited career he would pursue, which nice suburb his next smart girlfriend's parents would call home—they could afford to wait and wonder. The chance that I might be burned at the stake by crazed bikers was a whole new plane of unpredictability. It would be a near-miracle if they got through it without blaming me.

But I felt hopeful. I considered them capable of signs and wonders. They were both so smart and generous and not born yesterday.

Only after a few hours of lying sleepless did I realize that they might think (as the police did) that the bikers had been looking for Mark. He had badmouthed Grandpa Larry's friends to me, and most likely to others as well.

But if they had known he lived there, they would have said something. They had come there because they had seen my car and followed it. They had chased me because I moved, like wolves.

I gave the wolves two days to forget me and drove home unannounced. Mark was working late. Susan sat me down at the kitchen table and said my behavior was concerning. She looked a lot less upset than when she had implied that I was causing trouble in her marriage, so I knew where I stood.

I said, "I feel like this is unfair. It's not that I had scary guys after me—it's because I'm the kind of person who gets scary guys going after her, and now you've taken a step back from actually liking me, and the reason is I know scary guys, which wasn't exactly a secret when I showed up here!"

"We really like you, Bran," she said. "Those guys don't scare us. What worries us is this vocation you have for being a damsel in distress. It's a classic PTSD symptom to put your life on hold. To put it on repeat, acting out the trauma over and over, as a cry for help, you know?"

"Maybe it worked!" I said. "Me working full time after school every day of my life wasn't enough to get anybody's attention, was it? Maybe I needed to hit rock bottom. I mean it! The only good things that ever happened to me were when people intervened because they couldn't take it anymore."

"Rock bottom is a vulnerable position," she said. "It keeps the stakes high, because it's always about avoiding the worst." I perked up, because she sounded like Peter talking about *homo sacer*. Looking slightly offended by my look of cheer, she added, "Okay. It's like this. If you had a project or goal you were working toward, people could help you with that. People love helping each other. Look at your friend Peter, letting his fiancée's father get him into Harvard! But they want to do the easy stuff, not scrape pieces of you off the sidewalk."

"You're blaming me, like I thought you would," I said.

"No, I'm not."

"Since when are Bandidos after Peter? Nobody hates Peter!" I sniffled, smiling, and smeared away tears with the back of my hand. The idea of being hated by no one seemed enviably utopian.

"Of course nobody hates Peter," she said.

"And I wasn't passive. I ran away to Riverside and kept everybody safe. It's not like you want outlaw bikers in your life."

"Okay," she said. "That's fair. You don't need to be saved, and I'm sorry. I guess what you need is time, like Jay is getting. Time to be chaotic until you gel. You need to be in college like your friends. That's what I've been saying all along."

About half an hour after our conversation was over, I came back downstairs. She glanced at me and put her TV series on pause, and I said, "It occurred to me that maybe you do want outlaw bikers in your life, because actually nobody made you go to Bourdon Farms and steal my car."

She patted the sofa beside her, inviting me to sit down. When I did, she gave me a quick hug and said, "Listen to me, Bran. It's your car. We were afraid you would go get it. What we did had nothing to do with the car. It was *you*."

I hugged her back and cried. She reemphasized that she and Mark cared about me a lot, and I reminded her that my project was to become a screenwriter. She advised me to start telling everyone I knew that I was a screenwriter. I should say it over and over, regardless of context. It would take five years, but sooner or later someone who needed a screenwriter would think of me, and by then, I would know how to do it.

Back upstairs, I texted with Peter. He was usually so busy that the little exploratory texts I sent were not even answered, but on this particular evening he had time for me. I wrote that I had finally committed to my screenwriting project because at least it gave me an identity (screenwriter).

He replied, "Convenient! Feeling conflicted over that advice. Hollywood = compromise for failed writers turning 40. Read Bourdieu, Rules of Art." Before I could respond, he had added, "No wait fuck me you're Hollywood now, read Joseph Campbell Hero w/1k Faces $$$$$ jk."

My phone rang. "This really gets me," he said. "You shouldn't be writing to a formula so early in your career. Screenwriting leaves de facto zero latitude for creativity. It's like a programming language. Skip a beat, and it won't compile. It gets edited by committee, in rooms full of people, and they're all like speed-freak versions of Jay's friend Rick when he talks about his epic. I hate to think of you wasting your life."

"Compared to working in a coffee shop?"

"Please don't prostitute yourself. Not yet. Of course you should write. You were born for it. You have nothing. Movies cost millions to make. You can't even be a postcard painter like Hitler, without money to buy paint. But you can write if you own a pen and paper. The Romantics were writers because they were broke. The other option is movie actor, and the only Romantic hot enough was Shelley. Wordsworth was a dog, Keats had a schnozz, Byron limped—sorry—and Blake and Coleridge were hamsters. So was Leigh Hunt."

"Did you drink a lot of coffee?"

"I haven't slept in thirty hours, but no. I'm writing an article for a Festschrift, the academic version of a burnt offering in propitiation of the gods. There's a comp-lit deity retiring, and as a final gesture of his benevolence he might get me a contract for a monograph. You need to write, Bran, because if you don't, all the writers will be global jeunesse dorée, forced to choose between a career in the arts and yacht racing. Bourgeois bohemians who think they learned to write when they learned to speak. You need to start writing now, or you're going to put on the mask of gender and I'm going to look up one day and see your face on a billboard, advertising skin cream. If your audience cares how you look, it's sex work. That's why you need to write."

"You need to go to sleep. Please, Peter? You'll make yourself sick."

"Two more pages," he said.

The next day Susan and Mark agreed that I could continue living in their guest room while they kept their ears open for house-sitting opportunities. In the days to come, they expressed concern that I had no new friends from work. But if I had been less solitary, they would not have wanted me in their house. They certainly never complained about my lack of a partner. Their house was classic Proposition 13, a vintage wood-frame bungalow. It had a lot of rooms, but all of them were small, for a total of maybe twelve hundred square feet. Privacy was a shared convention. There was not really anywhere to hide.

In any case I was soon hardly ever there, because Jay drafted me into the two-person writing room of his personal screenwriting boot camp.

Peter was feeding him the same line about starting at the top, along with the relevant vocabulary, so he was going to be an auteur or nothing. Their first best idea was to build a portfolio of striking short films to launch Jay's career at the film school. It was highly competitive, but no movie experience was required for admission. Applicants were expressly enjoined from submitting films—a stipulation Peter found suspicious, one of those low thresholds institutions set for the sake of diversity so they can go on coddling industry scions in peace. At his urging, Jay was determined to matriculate armed with a reel as disconcerting as his dancing, but in a good way. We knew he would get in, because Peter would write the essays.

Jay had no way of producing films without me. Aspirants to the art of auteur cinema must, as a rule, be socially very much in demand. They require numerous subordinates with rare technical expertise to follow their instructions for hours on end, in exchange for one-line credits on films no one ever sees. Either that or they pay them. But he was decades away from coming into his inheritance. He needed me, and I had nothing better to do. As an aspiring screenwriter, I could chalk it up to experience, whether I learned anything or not.

For our first movie I spent three weeks at UCLA, sleeping on an air mattress on his floor. I needed no ID to get into the college buildings if I was with him. They tell students not to hold the door open for strangers, but if I claimed to have mislaid my student ID card, people would let me in anywhere, even the dorms.

The art of cinema proved to be mind-blowingly time-consuming, and not only because we had no idea what we were doing. Shooting thirty seconds took us two hours even at our most efficient. We had to arrange reading lamps, borrow panels from the drop ceiling as reflectors, hang bath towels over the windows, and hope like mad not to be interrupted, because we were making his film in his dorm's game lounge.

Jay's filmic visual acuity was a novel phenomenon, directly linked to his newfound horror of public ridicule. To avoid compounding artistic risk (the necessary gamble incumbent on all creativity) with social risk (gratuitous, avoidable self-torture), his work had to look super tight. As a filmmaker, he became a perfectionist in a way that had been impossible when he was performing live. It was analogous to the contrast between how I could write—when I had endless hours to do it in—and how I talked.

Writing dialogue was hard for me. If I copied the verbal tics of people I liked, it felt as though I were parodying them. If I parodied people I disliked, it reminded me of them, which I hated. But writing Jay's first movie was easy as pie, because instead of dialogue I used dialectics. All I had to do was channel the flat, shameless tone of the discourse of power. Once my crass speeches were written, we took turns reading them aloud, displaying bored reactions to the news that aliens had announced their intention to destroy Earth. The camera moved from Jay to me as if we thought we were conversing, but we gave no evidence of listening to each other. We did not act. Peter had described to each of us separately, over the phone, how the French director Robert Bresson had commanded his lead in *Un condamné à mort s'est échappé* not to act, and how the actor's expressionless demeanor had been hailed as a revolutionary masterpiece of dramatic subtlety. It took practice to stop performing, but after a while we could read our lines as if we were saying grace. Our themes were humiliation, degradation, dehumanization, defilement, destruction, and death. We called it *Dystopia: A Pre-Apocalyptic Revel*. Our apathy toward the aliens' plans presented onscreen as the most variegated shades of emotional devastation.

Video editing turned out to be the most fun part, once we figured out the software. Making sequences of partial gestures cohere into a drama through montage was straight-up flamenco, in formal terms, at least according to Peter.

Jay's filmiest course at that time was an introduction to visual culture for English majors. No longer naïve enough to put things online, he showed *Dystopia: A Pre-Apocalyptic Revel* to several students on his phone before class. It went over alarmingly well. No one believed he had made it, even though they could see him right there onscreen. Someone called the instructor over to watch it, and the beginning of class was delayed by ten minutes while they all watched it twice.

An hour after his premiere, Jay told me over the phone (I was back in Torrance) that the instructor had professed admiration for my talent, particularly after Jay had revealed that I was not a student. He had held my contact information back until he could ask me whether it was okay to reveal it. "Your teacher wants to meet me?" I said. "What for?"

"Beers and Rohypnol," Jay said, referring to the date-rape drug. "He asked me how old you are, and I said jailbait and that you don't look like that in real life, but he was still into it."

Our next short was called *White Flight* and featured no text at all, like a music video. I could be seen being gripped by panic as I realized I was surrounded by nonwhite students. The surreptitious setup scenes were a little too easy to get, since the Black and Asian students at UCLA liked to congregate in groups. I fled from hiding place to hiding place across campus, using survivalist skills Axel had taught me, blending in with bushes and stooping down low to peer around corners.

There was no escape, so I ran up to the roof of a skyscraper and jumped off, radiant with relief. It was super fascist. I was like Hitler dying in his bunker because he lost the war.

My suicide was easier to film than it sounds. I put my hand on the crash bar that led from Jay's dorm's fire stairs to the roof, emerged on top of a parking garage, stepped off a random carport onto my car ("guerrilla filmmaking"), and fell horizontally at the beach on a windy day with no clouds. Jay bought a cheap tripod, heavy enough to stand still in a stiff breeze, to keep the picture from wobbling. The soundtrack was pure Foley, homemade sound effects recorded in his room.

His classmates said that he was an artist and I was his muse. In reality, we were a team, and our muse was Peter. He cheered us on daily, assuring us that the more "professional" our work looked—the more it resembled advertising—the better a job we were doing of giving our fascist society what it wanted: the proliferation of social and cultural capital.

CHAPTER TEN

One day in May, while Jay and I were sitting in his dorm suite musing over his future at the film school, we hit a previously overlooked mission statement on the website that troubled us both. The institution was dedicated to promoting film that would inspire "social change." An alien invasion would bring about social change, and so might a rash of suicides among white students, but maybe not the kind they were talking about.

We texted Peter. It was impossible to predict whether he would respond, because sometimes he was in libraries for weeks at a time, or writing day and night, and often when he wasn't working he was eating—literally eating, with his mouth full of noodles. But he called right away, sounding relaxed, and Jay put him on speaker.

"Sure, you could do art that's not fascist," he said, "but you'd be dooming yourself to obscurity. It's the air we breathe. It's our only language. The way we fight racism under racism is by showing racism. The way we resist authority under authoritarianism is by provoking it to crush us. I mean others, obviously."

"But I want my films to be emancipatory," Jay said.

"What does that even mean? When a contemporary subject of a capitalist society talks about liberation, it's an instance of plagiarism, classically defined. Putting a concept to work after wrongfully abducting it. We can say 'liberation,' we can credit it to specific thinkers, but it's a concept that can't wait to slip its bonds and flee. It's never going to be happy with us." There was a sound as of the last traces of a milkshake being sucked up with a straw.

"What are you drinking?" Jay asked.

"Coffee bubble tea."

I said, "But you can't show liberation without showing the oppressor. You have to show fascism." I was trying to be clever, but also being entirely sincere. It seemed logical. How could people in emancipatory art be emancipated from nothing in particular? They had to be oppressed first.

"There's more to life than fascism," Peter said. "We could find things to fight against. Hunger, or disease. A lot of people have invested a lot of time in theorizing about life after the revolution. How we'll devote our time to enjoyment and progress, or regress to a preverbal state. There's plenty of source material for you out there, from Plato to Murray Bookchin. Not that the revolution has really panned out so far. It's more of a mythical paradise, like the Elysian Fields or the Big Rock Candy Mountain."

"Or Avalon," I said.

"You're a genius, Bran. Set a movie with a fascist visual aesthetic on Avalon. Unless it's been done. There's that Roxy Music record with the fascist cover. Hmm."

We gave him a moment to think.

"I would rather have it utopian from the start," Jay said. "Like, have an emancipatory visual aesthetic without the emancipation, like there were never any fascists. Just skip the fascist part."

"That's fascist already," Peter said. "Where are all your fascists now—in camps?"

"Okay, so it's swarming with fascists, but they don't have a language to express their fascism," Jay said. "Because their language only has one pronoun, 'I.' Like, if you think somebody smells bad, you have to say, 'I smell bad.' And then 'I need to do laundry.'"

"That's the distilled essence of fascism," Peter replied. "I loathe myself so soundly that I deserve death. I want to kill myself and all my selves over and over, until no one is left."

Jay paused and said, "I don't know." He picked up a paper clip from his desk, turned it over, and set it down again. I could see he was pondering a mile a minute and getting nowhere.

"Maybe they don't hate themselves," I suggested. "They just hate fascism. All their thoughts are fascist, but they know it, so they never do fascist stuff."

"Avalon is full of depressed, guilt-ridden fascists," Peter said.

"Yeah," I said. "That's right."

"Just moping around all day."

"They shouldn't be happy in paradise. It wouldn't be fair." I imagined the Hendersons as depressives—a huge improvement—and felt certain that I was right.

"Is it any emancipatory?" Jay asked. (He was making fun of my old boss at the coffee shop, who routinely used "any" before adjectives other than "good.")

"Yes, absolutely," Peter said. "I would live in that world."

Our progressive-activist movie for social change was a mix of my ideas and Jay's. First the title *Avalon* appeared over an extreme close-up of wavelets on the beach with the colors tweaked into gold, set to audio samples of gunfire. A sailboat, or rather a model belonging to Jay's father, could be seen departing into the sunset. We pulled it with monofilament fishing line from both sides to keep ourselves from appearing in the frame. For the remainder, we used the bluff by the lighthouse in Palos Verdes, which was the closest thing we could find to a green hill. The parks in L.A. had great hilltops, but there was nothing growing there but scrub. The golf courses were green but flat. At the lighthouse, they had watered the lawn without grading it. We arranged some red apples under the trees and filmed ourselves using the heavy tripod. I wore Susan's wedding dress. She and Mark had gotten married barefoot on the beach, so her dress was two layers of gauze with the top one open at the sides, like an ancient Greek peplos worn over a chiton. Jay was my consort, in a revealing chlamys made from two yards of white muslin. We dubbed in the sound later. It started with synthesizers and tinkling bells. Jay kneeled on the rug that was a precondition for my borrowing the dress (understandably, Susan did not want grass stains on it) while I walked uphill with the sun behind me, hair glowing and body visible in silhouette. I opened my mouth. What came out was agonized screaming (not my screaming; we stole it from horror movies). He replied with four parallel tracks of choral singing (also pirated). I replied with more screaming and some singing, and he replied with singing and a touch of screaming. We never formed words, just opened our mouths for a few seconds at a time. Meanwhile, we looked off in various directions, struck ambiguously moody poses, or turned to face each other. We were having a conversation, and with every exchange we came closer to sharing a language. Our movements remained slow, in deference to our membership in the postrevolutionary leisure class. In the end, we touched hands and the screaming gave way to all singing, all the time.

If it had not looked and sounded cool, it would have been mega laughable, but its professionalism was tight as a drum. Jay made sure of it, adjusting the sound and color, frame by frame, with expensive filter software, over the course of torturous weeks.

He promised to tell me how the faculty reacted. I would have liked to keep following him around campus, but there was no way I could keep shadowing him in exclusive courses with expensive equipment. The film school would notice an extra person.

With Mark's tacit assent, I had continued caring for his and Susan's yard after they returned from their Easter vacation. I asked him whether he minded. Looking away, he abashedly said that it seemed like a fair trade for room and board. Susan seemed more at ease with it, in part because he assuaged his guilt with extra housework. Plus, it was the same deal they had with their son: you sleep and eat, you mow. Weeks later, during the *Avalon* editing phase, when Jay's family's gardener got taken by ICE from his night job at a warehouse, I made a deal with Esme to replace him. Jay's neighbor then saw me over the wall and asked whether I would like to work for her as well. By the time *Avalon* went online, I was devoting two days a week to maintaining lawns and vacuuming pools for cash.

This was not quite the same as drafting a feature screenplay. It made for tension at home. Mark and Susan had taken in an ugly duckling and bargained for a swan, not a better-looking duck—that is, a college girl who would sprout wings and fly away, not a working-class lodger. I strove to be less noticeable around the house. Our interactions became somewhat formalized. They started asking me whether I planned to eat dinner. I kept a coffee mug in my room and washed it by hand instead of taking a clean one every time.

I occasionally thought of packing the car and moving to Entradero Park.

I could halt that kind of ideation by reminding myself that it was not my job to throw me out. It was their job—theirs alone!—and any annoyances I occasioned them, up to their breaking point, were their problem, not mine. Being a burden was a novelty I struggled to conceptualize, but I sensed that it was a key life skill I needed to learn.

My fight to root out the Protestant work ethic from my soul became culture clash only when I visited my grandparents. I presented myself (and they consequently saw me) as my generous landlords' humble live-in groundskeeper. My having time for two additional clients was a good sign, evidence that they were not exploiting me unduly. It was my role to be taken advantage of, if ideally only slightly, and not my employers'. My exploiting an employer—robbing him of the profits due him under capitalism—would have been as dishonorable to them as shoplifting. So I was not about to tell them I had a brass bed facing the sunrise and full refrigerator access in exchange for biweekly mowing.

Jay began his life as a cineaste by buying us two memberships to the American Cinematheque. He studied the programs of art house movie theaters and watched their trailers online. But he also enrolled in two courses per summer session at the film school, including digital cinematography and historical survey courses that entailed homework, and his schedule was soon a sclerotic muddle. That entire summer, we saw maybe ten big-screen movies and attended one reception, where he shook the hand of a famous cameraman neither of us had ever heard of.

After the regular semester got going in October, he had no time left for me. He returned calls and responded to texts days later, the way Peter did. I tried telling myself that it was because I had been an adequate best friend for a dilettante and not for a man with a life, but the film school was hardly designed for people with lives. Fitting a non-fellow-student into his daytime schedule would have required logistical superpowers. To speak with him for an hour, I would have had to wait outside each college building like a dog, walk him to his next class, and spread the conversation over the course of two days in twelve five-minute snippets.

His nights were taken. Iñaki, an *osito* (bear cub), had taken his fancy the very first day. In the pictures Jay sent me, long curly hairs sprouted out of every gap in his clothing, including cuff plackets and buttonholes. Iñaki's métier was screenwriting— not a perfect match for Jay's supposed auctorial ambitions, but not in direct conflict, either. Iñaki had liaised with an aspiring actor named Rory, regarding Jay as a passable "twink" while revering Rory's classic good looks. Rory valued Iñaki's fur, but not as much as he treasured Jay's elfin physique. Within days, their lust triangle had become a threesome, and Jay had gone from having no sex at all to having all the sex in the world.

Presumably, with one another they talked about school projects and other cool stuff. Jay was increasingly proficient at looking cool, which entailed acting cool. He communicated with me mostly to unload his remaining nerdy, naïve, anxious, or romantic thoughts. He said he was in love with Iñaki, but that Rory had "the dick of death." I did not ask him what he meant.

He was in his suite only seldom. If I had moved in there, I could have seen more of him without getting in his way, but our interaction would still have been measured in seconds per week. Beyond his thrilling sex life, he had committed himself to what was surely the most time-consuming mode of artistic performance ever invented in the history of the world. Traditionally, film production was slow as molasses in January. Workers spent entire careers staring into space, waiting their turns to apply makeup or load the Steadicam or whatever. At UCLA, slowness was being actively reinvented by students brandishing late-model iPhones who desired pressure-cooker-style training under conditions of real-world precarity in direct competition with one another. If the courses were too easy, the weak would not fail and the strong would not prevail. They had designed and refined a parallel creative culture for the sake of slowing one another down.

Jay had to choose, and he chose success—that is, to forget about me and Peter as if we had been ships that passed in the night. He devoted his thoughts to Iñaki and Rory, colleagues he barely knew and with whom he was basically having the same one-night stand over and over.

Or maybe Jay stopped talking to me because I was boring. I was marking time, and Peter was far, far away. His movements never took him west of Wellesley. We sometimes texted while he was riding the bus up to Maine to see his family. He mused on life and recommended books and authors for me to look up.

Surfing a term like "Klaus Theweleit" or "Xavière Gauthier" can give you a long ride.

Occasionally, he emailed me in the middle of the night, things like "I miss you so much. You're the best thing in my life, the only thing standing between me and the void. What are you doing right now? Want to talk?" I was always sleeping, and he must have known it. Was I being fucked with, or what? It was too obvious.

I cracked once and wrote back over breakfast, "I'm in love!!!! When will I see you????" His answer was a meandering rundown of undergraduate conferences on the West Coast at which he might be invited to present papers. He said he was on the case. But in the meantime, he had no reason to come to California, and I had no way of getting to New England. I had money, a little, enough for a plane ticket to Boston. But what would I do when I got there—have dinner with him and Yasira? He had moved three thousand miles away. He was marrying her. Why was it so hard for me to believe we would not be spending our lives together? How do you define spending a life together? Why could I not take my hand off the hot stove?

I can tell you why not: because burning up is too fucking pleasant.

The day before Thanksgiving, Jay came home, sans boyfriends, and we finally had time to talk. Iñaki was doing his homework for him. They were supposed to plot movie scripts. The assignment was weeks old, and Jay and Rory were still empty-handed, but since Iñaki had spare ideas, he was writing up extras.

We lay on loungers by the pool, wearing street clothes, peeling and eating organic mandarin oranges from a basket Esme had left there for us, and I asked him why he was letting Iñaki submit plots in his name.

"They're not looking for ideas like yours and mine," he said. "I have no clue how you inspire social change. Iñaki has it down cold."

"Did they say yet which social change?"

"No, of course not!"

I asked what Iñaki's ideas were like.

"The one he's writing for me is about sex workers unionizing, or winning the right to be regarded as employees of an online platform and get paid sick leave, by picketing their headquarters or something."

"Did he do the one for Rory yet?"

"Yeah. It's about fishermen whose fish are going extinct."

I asked what Iñaki was writing for himself.

"There's this boy," Jay said, "like ten years old, who's worried about Mexican kids getting separated from their parents when they sneak into the U.S. through the desert. He hears about these two little girls that are stuck out alone in the wilderness, so he runs away to help them out. His parents are totally having panic attacks, and so is their mom. But they die . . ." His voice trailed off.

"How does it end?"

"There's a reunion scene between him and his parents."

"Is it any emancipatory?"

"Fuck no!" he said. "It's like a steel cage match between kitsch and fascism. And everybody goes home happy, because the Mexican kids die and the white kid doesn't."

"Did you tell Iñaki that?"

"No. I love Iñaki. But in my plot, he makes out like flat-rate sex work is a happy ending. And fishermen versus extinction is balls-out fascist! There's man versus man, man versus nature, man versus society, and man versus self, right? This is none of the above. It's the workingman against the big bully, global heating. We know how that ends up!"

"Homo sacer," I said, smiling because Jay had not forgotten Peter after all.

"The professor worships Iñaki."

"I thought you were the one in love with him."

"Yeah, but we don't have long conversations like I did with Peter. It's incredible sex, that's all."

We peeled some oranges and watched towhees pick through leaf litter under the pomegranate trees. Jay turned his head to the sun and I noticed that he was starting to get crow's-feet. He looked thinner.

"What's in it for Iñaki?" I said. "I mean, him doing your homework."

"He gets feedback on all three ideas, and if one of them gets to the next round, he can write it. We're producing a film next semester."

"You should write your own plot," I said. "Your ideas are so much better."

"But they're abstract. You can't inspire social change with a bunch of metaphors. It has to be realistic. Except his ideas are secretly metaphors, because it's like the social change is that there are no boundaries anymore and people are free to sell endangered fish or their own bodies. It's a metaphor for free markets—oh my God. You know what I just realized? The social change they want is fucking *libertarianism*!" He quivered with amusement, giggling but without making any sound, as though he were under orders never to laugh at Iñaki.

"Grandpa Larry was a libertarian."

"Is it any emancipatory?"

"It sounds like it ought to be, but I sure don't think so," I said.

He called Peter, who immediately picked up. "Jay!" Peter said.

Jay put him on speaker and asked, "Do you have a minute?"

"What's up? I'm writing."

"I was just sitting here with Bran and we were wondering. Is libertarianism emancipatory?"

"Anything else would violate the dystopian narrative. The best we can do is exempt individuals from the rule of law. Putting new laws in place would be utopian."

"So . . ." Jay hesitated. "Is it?"

"You want to find out how you can tweak speculative utopias to make them palatable to your social-justice-warrior film school, and I think with libertarianism you're on the right track. Without breaking the dominant narrative, I think you could, for instance, write about decentralized, autonomous organizations that feed the homeless without a license or build them houses that aren't to code. Make your heroes outlaws and then crush them under the iron heel of the state. Think *Gladiator,* but like Zola. Unless you want to hazard your career, which I wouldn't advise. Film has to advertise itself because it's expensive to produce. Okay, sorry, I have to go. See you soon—bye!"

It was a strange way to sign off, since we had not seen each other in a year and had no current plans to do so. My phone dinged with a text from him. "Sorry no time to say how much I want you, besides Jay doesn't need to hear it," he wrote. It made me cry, so I got up and walked over to the oleanders to blow my nose and think of a reply.

Jay said, "Who texted you?"

I said, "Nobody you know." I was thinking, Nobody I know, either.

Jay invited me to student parties off campus on the following two Saturdays. He warned me to keep my screenwriting identity under my hat. "We all share all our ideas all the time," he explained. "Because we know who came up with what first, they have dibs. But your ideas would be fair game, because you wouldn't be there to call dibs."

The first party was sparsely attended, because a different and better party was taking place in some other apartment. Even Jay was annoyed to be there. Iñaki and Rory left soon after we arrived, saying they were getting something to eat, and never came back. After two hours, I went to Jay's room to sleep.

The second party was in a house off campus that seven students shared. The people there looked interesting and alluring, but they were too high to talk to me. I mean high in a social sense—*bon chic, bon genre* filmmakers, talking about the right career moment to apply for a Guggenheim, while I was merely myself. Nothing I could say made me sound like a useful contact. No matter what people were talking about when I walked up, some man in the group would soon ask where I lived. After a while, rooms seemed to fall silent when I entered.

After several futile attempts to speak to people other than Jay, I decided to suggest we both leave. I approached him and Iñaki and saw that I would be leaving alone. Jay was draped against him, nestled into his chest, making himself shorter, with a posture and expression I had never seen before. I said, "Having fun?"

Iñaki raised his glass and said, "I wouldn't be here if I weren't."

Jay raised cold eyes to me and said, "Bran would."

It was the meanest thing he had ever said to anyone in my presence, and it had been said directly to me, and in front of Iñaki, his partner, as though he wanted to prove he was over me or something. It was too nuts. I left the party and drove home to Torrance.

In his defense, he never remembered saying it. He even apologized, not that it helped. The clotting factor for wounds like that is reassurance, and he could not even confirm that it had happened.

Iñaki flew home for Christmas. His family lived on a ranch in Montana, and he looked forward to cross-country skiing and hot tubs and riding horses in the snow and other things that sounded extremely romantic, even to me.

Jay dangled for an invitation as if he had been his fiancé. He had romanticized the lack of romance in their relationship as something especially romantic—a ruling sexual passion— but apparently that was not something Iñaki needed, not when there were landscapes to conquer, or horses to currycomb, or the men of Montana, or whatever.

I pointed out how cold it would have been. Jay almost sobbed describing the shearling overcoats and mittens Iñaki would have lent him. He was in the grip of a new and different insanity, like nothing I had ever seen. Rory, too, had gone home (Austin), leaving Jay with no sexual outlet whatsoever. He downloaded a dating app and spent hour after hour left-swiping everybody, including men who looked exactly like Iñaki. It was a deliberate exercise of magic. Phones could not transmit exclusive sexual chemistry. If he had right-swiped on an Iñaki and gotten a match, it would have proved that he was a superficial Californian.

CHAPTER ELEVEN

Peter called me after Christmas dinner, while I was watching a movie with Susan, Mark, and Will. I went to the kitchen and pulled the sliding door closed.

"I miss you," he said. "I'm on Martha's Vineyard with the Yasira clan. It's freezing cold and windy. She won't wear a hat. She got bronchitis. I'm on the beach by myself. Can you hear the wind? I have my hood pulled down over my head and the phone and it's dark as a cave in here. I keep thinking of you."

"That's so nice," I said.

"'And stuck together, facing the terrible splendor, we silently lift our eyes. Those are the distant islands, the high worlds we saw in dreams, that made us live under the entire sky and made our lives hell.' That's from a poem by the Zionist poet Bialik. He wrote it in modern Hebrew before modern Hebrew was a language."

"Avalon is Palestine?" I said. I was deliberately keeping my sentences short. I did not want to look back on this call and remember my own voice.

"I love you."

"That's good to hear." I said it with an extra dollop of stupidity because he had made a warm, ecstatic feeling engulf my heart and brain. He was silent, so I added, "You make me happy. I can hear the wind a little bit."

"There are billions of grains of sand here," he said.

"I bet!"

"There are eight billion people on earth, like grains of sand, and then there's you and me."

"I love you, too." My voice got very low, a sultry whisper I had never heard from myself before. I sounded like a singer, or someone in an old movie.

"So what I wanted to say is"—long pause—"I'm coming to California April sixth. Stanford comp lit runs one of these pandering pseudo-academic conference-festivals where they invite creative writing teachers who moonlight as writers to read their work and lecture on poetics for the general public as a marketing tactic to their own trustees to create a nimbus of contemporary relevance for their research programs, and one of the guests of honor is Italian. They were looking for someone with good Italian to be his doyenne, as if he can't order food or find the bathroom in America without help. So anyway, I'd been in touch with the organizers because I might do my graduate work there, and I got myself in the door, all expenses paid, because I've written about him. I'll be around nearly a week. Do you think you could make it up there? It would be good for you, I think, to meet writers."

Struggling to process so much information at once, I asked how I would meet writers.

"It's like this," he said. "I won't have a lot of spare time during the conference. But I can get you invited to the after-party at Drew Miller's place in Santa Cruz. It's notorious, this party. You should bring Jay. Miller is a creative writing teacher with a cult following. Might be really good for you to know."

I backtracked enough to ask, "Are you bringing Yasira?"

"She loves the Bay Area. Her mother might come, too."

"That doesn't sound . . ." My voice slowed a bit.

"I know, I know. Skip Palo Alto. But you have to come to this party! It goes all night. Nobody leaves. I can't get you a guest room, but there's definitely room for you somewhere. It's eight acres with redwoods. We can find a place to be alone together, whether Yasira's there or not. She hasn't made up her mind. I want to see you alone. It's important."

I immediately called Jay. My mind was racing, repeatedly crashing into—of all things—the questionable reliability of my car. The engine had chugged around L.A. for years without major incident, and the wheels were where they belonged, with the brakes attached, but the idea of tackling four hundred miles each way gave me pause. Going to Santa Cruz in Jay's BMW sounded a lot more realistic, as though we might actually arrive. Also, transportation was a reassuringly tangible concern compared with a nebulous third-party invitation that might unravel if I touched it.

"I don't think I can," Jay said. "April is when we produce our feature. On the sixth I might still be in Vegas. We're filming the desert scenes with the dead kids in some off-road-vehicle recreation area, and they need my car because it's four-wheel drive. It sucks, because it would be awesome to see Peter."

"He says this party will be full of high-powered writers."

"But not movie people. Anyway, you should fly. Just fly to San Jose and catch a bus. It's like a hundred bucks. Maybe you can't fly without photo ID. I don't know. I never tried."

"I've never been up there before," I said. "I've never even been to Malibu."

"God, I wish I had time to take you. Sorry I didn't tell you before, but I'm directing."

I was stunned. "That's amazing!"

"I know. They love my visual sense and my spinelessness about everything else."

"So what," I said. "As long as your name is on it. Who's playing the kids?" I knew the adult roles would be taken by acting students at the film school.

"Actors," he said. "You can't throw a rock in Westwood without hitting a ten-year-old actor. Then when the Mexican girls are dead, it's clothes and wigs, facedown, with sticks inside, to make them look extra emaciated."

"That's so fascist."

"I know," he said. "I love it. But I was wondering. I had this idea. If you wrote a script for me—I mean for me to submit in my advanced screenwriting workshop—it would get me out of writing it, and you could get feedback without anybody stealing your idea, because they would all think it was mine. I can't be an auteur filmmaker without scripts, but seriously, I do not have time to write some feature-length movie right now. I'm supposed to be having fun in Jackson Hole for two weeks with Mom and Pop, and then I'm responsible for producing and directing Iñaki's thing!"

I said yes. He cheerfully appended a confession that he had known the assignment was coming for at least a year.

He flew to Wyoming the next day, and I got to work expanding *Dystopia: A Pre-Apocalyptic Revel* into a pilot for a TV series. It took me two weeks. Because the story was dystopian— tacitly fascist—it seemed to write itself. All I had to do was open my mind and channel the culture.

The writing process reminded me of the books of Buddhist

precepts Mom's Rinpoche sold in his gift shop. I observed my inner state with ritual humility, neither judging nor generalizing, radically honoring dystopia. I breathed pure mind, which was neither cerebral, loving, nor material, but a background hum of dystopia that was always with me, like the sky. This script oozed from me like molten gold.

Idyllic, late-capitalist Earth, a place populated by whiners who basically had no problems compared to what was coming, had become the battlefield in a turf war between opposing gangs of space aliens—mercenaries hired by mining companies, à la Pinkertons—who were instantly sympathetic because they shared a relatable desire to win their war. They whizzed around in formation in fighter spaceships, looking cool. The human characters were instantly sympathetic because they were collateral damage. The egalitarian masses died without regard to nationality, color, or creed. There was no danger that viewers would get them mixed up with the aliens, who were from a heavier planet (Jupiter) and looked like orange amoebae ten feet in diameter—flattened at home, blobs in low gravity, spherical in outer space, but always safety orange and way too big. Jupiter was an amorphous place in which all organisms, unintelligent or not, floated like grease on soup. Its industry had initially relied on the enslavement of a lower class to extract heavy elements from the lethally hot planetary core, but advances in technology allowed the amoebae to mine minerals from moons and nearby planets without risking workers' lives. Earth was valued for its salts. Its ecosystems did not interest them so much, although they sometimes brought back individual organisms to display in diorama-like habitats in a pressurized dome on Ganymede. There, a woman was confined to a glassine sphere ten feet in diameter, incessantly voiding diarrhea, lying nude on a drain like a sexy patient in an S&M cholera ward. She got nothing to eat or drink but soybeans and corn syrup, which the amoebae had understandably concluded were humanity's staple foods. During opening hours her cage was engulfed on all sides by an undulating mass of orange amoebic tourists pressing their eye spots to the surface. Only when the zoo closed could she see two neighboring spheres. One contained a flock of sparrows, the other a young elephant that had been captured as a baby and could no longer move. The surviving humans on Earth—defiant, orphaned, in rags—preached a cult of pragmatic kindness. "Death absolute is the truth of our existence as a whole," their leader said wisely at one point, stanching her dying son's wounds in the ruins of Westminster Abbey. Fortunately, progressive amoebae, inspired by news footage of the zoo to regard colonialism skeptically, had developed a plan to preserve Earth for future generations of tourists. One of them embedded with the mercenaries, repeatedly breaking ranks to experience Earth's living wonders, such as recordings of music. The amoebae had no need of recording equipment, because they could communicate memories to one another by touching pseudopods. As the pilot episode ended, the survivors received a message of hope. The embedded amoeba poked a pseudopod through a tiny aperture in its spaceship right into the human leader's temporal lobe—as fast as it could, to keep from popping—leaving her aphasic and bleeding. In a flash, she learned that there are nice amoebae on Jupiter, it learned English, and episode two stepped into the on-deck circle.

Dystopia was a tour de force of degradation, dehumanization, defilement, destruction, and satiric obviousness. I sent it to Peter on a Thursday night. He got back to me by text on Saturday afternoon. "Genocide w/o antifa polit distractions. Love it!!!!"

I wrote back, "Is it any emancipatory."

"Emancipatory = show for aliens to convince them humans worth saving," he texted. "We master their arts learn mitosis grow pseudopods etc. see also Forster, A Passage to India."

After making a few tweaks and polishing the dialogue a bit, I sent the script to Jay. He replied five days later.

"OMG OMG," he wrote. "I will SLAY with this. This will be OPTIONED."

I wriggled, basking in the light of my fabulousness. In the eyes of my friends, I was already one of the monsters in *Monster.*

I took up reading my script aloud to myself, revising and revising until there was no conflict I had not heightened, no emotion I had not honed.

In parallel, to keep from losing my mind, I began a script set on Avalon. The entire population was royalty, like in the frontispiece of Hobbes's *Leviathan,* knights and ladies leading public lives of august chastity with private lives off-camera, and the script centered on a rustic girl knight who wanted to bottle-feed an orphaned sea otter. She had to put in for the milk at a round-table meeting because there was so little milk on agrarian, communist Avalon—only what the foals and fawns left over (there were no goats or sheep, to spare the vegetation, and no cows, to keep the meadows nice)—and it was spoken for long in advance. A chivalrous friend donated his milk ration, helping her feed the otter until it was weaned. Then they returned it to its colony, where, watched over by vegetarian orcas, it frolicked and ate marine snails.

I thought, If I were an alien, would this convince me to save humanity? And I realized that it would not, because only a fascist alien would want to destroy humanity in the first place.

I turned the orcas back into vicious apex predators. The heroine risked death, defending the otters from them with her sea kayak and a spear. The fascist in me loved her more than ever. The fascist in me wanted to save her.

While devoting myself full time to my craft or sullen art (*Dystopia* was my craft; *Return to Avalon* was my art), I took on an additional gardening gig with an elderly friend of Mark's. He had retired from his job defending the city from personal-injury cases and hoped to reduce expenses by replacing his lawn with a rock garden and some aridity-tolerant ground cover. He had leg trouble and could not squat or kneel.

He liked to talk to me while I worked. He said his opponents had lived by two mottos: "You give me damages and I'll find liability" and "Man got hurt, man gotta get paid." His funny stories were about people who had neither suffered damages nor gotten hurt. His bitter stories were about people whose damages and injuries were not the city's fault. He was telling me about an uninsured texting driver who plowed through a group of people on a crosswalk, all of whom sued the city, when I heard Harleys approaching.

"I need something from the garage," I said, flitting into the building.

From behind his car I could see at least ten bikers ride slowly by, most without helmets, carrying American and Confederate flags. I recognized Country, Loki, and guys named Ramblin' Man and Damien. The retired lawyer stood at attention and saluted.

After I came back out, I asked him why he had saluted.

"Because I'm slower on my feet than you are."

"I know those guys," I said. "They were good friends with Larry Henderson, and they hate me."

"Then thanks for hiding," he said.

Since I spent entire days outdoors, doing my yard gigs rain or shine, there was not a lot Susan or Mark could say to fault my work habits. I had never shown them my writing, saying it was too amateurish to be read by anyone but students—which it surely was—but they knew that I spent a lot of time typing.

They knew it for a fact, because they disrespected my privacy. Susan would knock while opening my door to ask me whether I wanted anything to eat or drink. I worked sitting at a vanity with my back to her, so she could see that I was typing in a document.

Over dinner one night, she asked whether I would like the two of them to read my script, perhaps as a dramatic table reading. It could be fun, and might even help me.

In a moment of mental weakness, I replied that it would be workshopped at UCLA soon enough.

"I don't get it," Mark said.

"I do," Susan said. "She's doing Jay's homework!"

"Bran, you should not—" he began, but she stopped him.

"People have been doing Jay's homework all his life, and

I can't say it ever hurt any of them," she said. "It's certainly helped him!"

"Well, if you look at it that way," Mark said. "But is it fair?"

"He's not going to steal my script," I said. "If somebody wanted to option it for money, it would totally stop mattering to him what grade he got in that class. He's my friend."

Emotionally, I was a cruise missile directed at the hills above Santa Cruz—not yet launched, but inwardly preparing. It did not seem like a long wait to see Peter. I had not been near him in almost a year and a half, since our hotel weekend with the trip to Joshua Tree. Another month or two was nothing. I felt as though I could have held my breath, or taken a nap, and the party in Santa Cruz would have started.

He sent me the details of the invitation in mid-March. The conference ended on a Friday. The party was Saturday after-noon, the eleventh of April, beginning at four-thirty. That gave people time to get there from Palo Alto and rest up, but also winnowed out the ones who were in a rush to be someplace else after the conference. A subtle structural forcing was also in evi-dence, according to him. On Saturdays in April, many people in the vicinity of age thirty had weddings to fly to, so the party was heavy on people of other ages, that is, students and forty-plus.

With the address in hand, I found my vague imaginings could now be underpinned with fuzzy aerial views of the prop-erty, painstakingly reconciled with the snippets of large-scale topographic maps that were available online. I studied digital snapshots until I could sense the aroma of northern seaside veg-etation and dank evergreen-forest mists. The property had outbuildings. There was a barn, which surely had a hayloft, into which he and I would climb to revisit whatever strange thing it was that we had. It might be for three minutes, but I was living for those three minutes.

Sometimes I managed to slip into a retrospective view and make fun of myself for feeling such anticipation, but never enough to stop myself from feeling it.

While indulging such reflections, I edged walks, vacuumed pools, arduously revised *Dystopia,* and deleted and restored *Return to Avalon* over and over. To do justice to the inadvertently sadistic aliens, I had to think through the implications of reinventing nature. To do justice to courageous communist royalty, I had to reinvent society as a lawmaker. The latter—utopian political world-building—was a lot harder. It was like fantasizing upstream, against the current.

In April, I finally told Mark and Susan about the party. They strongly encouraged me to go. "Don't be shy," Mark said. "It's a lucky break. Being introduced to serious writers could be a turning point in your life."

"And Drew Miller!" Susan said. "His stories are brilliant, and he's so famous. I'm impressed with your friend Peter for getting you invited there."

I was tempted to dress up, but she assured me that party clothes were unnecessary and inadvisable. If I felt conspicuous, I might have an out-of-body experience, seeing myself through imaginary skeptics' eyes, and freeze up like a bunny. She helped me pick out a dark-green sweater to wear with high-waisted jeans and ankle boots. "The key is keeping them clean until you get there," she said. "Don't put on any of this stuff until you can see the house."

The next day, she provided additional stern tips: "If you're worried about what you look like, don't waste time wondering. Find a mirror! If you feel lonely, do the same thing. Humans need eye contact and smiling. What people did before the invention of mirrors, I don't know."

I felt like saying, "But I do." I had discovered mirrors way too late in life.

I did not tell Fifi, Henry, or Will about my project. I did not want to loft this particular weak screwball into their strike zones. They would have batted me out of the park. I left it up to Jay.

Also, I no longer cared what they thought. Their treatment of me had become impersonal. They had stopped identifying with me, if they had ever started. They had no excess subjectivity to waste. They had paired off, and their time was devoted to the age-old challenge of jockeying two minds in two heads, with no room for a fifth wheel and no need. I had a right to aspire to the same utopian condition. I would stake what resources I had, so meager they were almost nudity. I would risk it all, risking almost nothing, because, unlike everybody else I knew, Peter wanted me trailing clouds of glory and nothing else. I was pretty sure of it. Almost confident.

The trip was planned over countless hours of absentminded visualization. I packed all my money, a brand-new sleeping bag, selected clothing, toiletries, towels, paper towels, water, bread, peanut butter, a box of Grape-Nuts, a bowl, a spoon, cookies, and a bag of pears. I would rely on gas station convenience stores for milk and microwave burritos. My spontaneous command of trip logistics made me feel masterful, as if the fire inside me were a cool blue flame. There was, as a matter of fact, no impulsive, impassioned way for me to get from Torrance to Santa Cruz. I could not exactly jog there. Maybe there were billionaires who could have rung for their helicopter pilots in a situation like mine, but my best option was the Mazda.

Mark had made me promise to take California State Route One, the two-lane, coastal version of the PCH. "Every Californian should drive it once," he said. "It's our patrimony." I agreed, partly because when the Mazda hit sixty miles an hour, which happened seldom enough in L.A., it began vibrating in an unsettling fashion. I wanted a stop-and-go road. Also, I had heard rude bikers—not just saps like Mark—celebrate the glories of Route One. It had to be the kind of unsubtle beauty that comes out and slugs you in the face.

My party plan crystallized to its tactical essence. Dressed like a rural cat burglar in inconspicuous blue and green, I would sneak in from the road, locate my quarry, beckon him away from whatever group he was entertaining in his function as provocateur, and then what? In all honesty, what?

gave myself four days to make the drive, leaving on the Wednesday before. Coffee-table books in the public library had made the stations of the route look so beautiful (not every road has its own coffee-table books!) that I wanted to be able to stop at every single one. Also, the Mazda had a habit of going to the cusp of overheating and staying there, and I did not want to put it to the test.

I rushed hesitantly—the traffic was such that no vehicle could really rush—past the Channel Island ports, and barged aggressively through the first suburban hundred miles chocka-block with towns and resorts, but when the headlands opened up and the ocean took on mass, my speed fell to a whisper. Soon I was harmonizing with an endless convoy of RVs, all making the leisurely drive together. When bikers appeared in my rearview mirror, I slowed to let them pass. They made my hands unsteady on the wheel, but most were clean-cut retirees on Hondas.

It was tiring to be behind boxy tanks constantly braking, so I parked the car once an hour or so on the edge of the road or in a driveway, standing at the guardrails to look down on shuttered houses and narrow beaches littered with shells and kelp.

I had planned to take longer breaks, but the unconscious

urge to put distance between myself and Torrance was stronger. On the first day, I put in almost two hundred miles.

That night I slept parked up a random side road, on the edge of an overgrazed pasture.

As much as I had talked about sleeping in my car, I had only done it in the desert. When I closed the windows against the dew and bugs, they fogged up within minutes. It must have been easy to see that there was a person inside. Before I fell asleep, folded up on the backseat, I felt extraordinarily cold. But although there were houses nearby and cars passing, no one bothered me, and in the morning the birds reminded me of the four overlaid tracks of choral singing in *Avalon*.

I arrived in Morro Bay, my first planned destination, at high tide and walked the causeway to its monolith, wafted on a feeling of elemental oneness. Morro Rock is a plutonic orb of inconceivable mass. I had never seen anything so large or so stubbornly itself. It was a cross between a sacred site and a dubious role model.

The air over the lagoon was thick with salt spray and mist that blurred the promenading birds and made the fluorescent windsurfing sails look pastel. I zigzagged, drawn both to the beach and to a cluster of RVs parked near the base of the causeway. Several had awnings that made them look like food trucks.

Driving onward, I soon stopped to eat a burrito, leaning on my hatchback in the convenience store parking lot.

A few miles on was a marsh full of pintails—pretty ducks with long, sleek necks, all jockeying for position and barking softly in a light shower of rain. It was so nice to look at that I parked the car again, thinking of taking another walk. Then I thought better of it (no umbrella) and drove on.

I was glad to be headed north. The road was curvy and distracting, with only two lanes, both of them narrow, further straitened by rock slides and crumbling shoulders. The lightweight travel trailers fishtailed in every gust of wind, probably making the white-knuckled drivers feel alive. They braked suddenly for overlooks and made adventurous U-turns. Going north put me on the landward side. If anyone ran me off the road, my car might get scratched up against an embankment, but I would not slide noisily into the Pacific.

I coasted past Hearst Castle, a crypto-fascist dream house where everyone else seemed to be stopping, and parked again near a beach full of elephant seals. They were molting, shedding skin in patches and shreds. Like Morro Rock, elephant seals are very much themselves, at one with their essential natures. It would be depressing to imagine them any other way. Imagine not wanting to eat raw squid until you weigh a ton, not wanting to live in a harem and get raped, but having no choice, because your identity (basic elephant seal) determines you. One must assume they are happy beings, like rocks and fires. But what if they hate it? Who ever said being was supposed to be fun?

The other nights I slept in state park campgrounds. They cost money, but were safer than waysides—probably—and had showers. They lay tucked into shadowy glens, at human scale, a chance to wash off dust and wonder at the tininess of my scrubbed ears and toes. The immensity of the landscape was making me tiny, physically. But I knew (or know?) no more reassuring feeling to have while alone, sick as that sounds: a world full of grandeur, and myself unnoticed, a flying eyeball.

On I drove, with frequent pauses. To my left were long, grassy meadows dotted with cattle, leading to distant ranch buildings and lighthouses behind which chasms dropped to the ocean—nameless tableaux with numbered addresses, repeated around every curve—not scenic highlights, much less public parks. To my right, long and enticing rutted roads scattered with cascading stones burrowed into the hills. I wanted to spend months walking all of them. Stopping at an overlook, I saw pelicans in an endless column, soaring north to Oregon or Alaska or wherever it is that pelicans look for work. They were visibly broke, airborne *Lumpen,* but flowing free as the air. From a picnic table at a roadside café I texted Peter, "Made it to Big Sur."

American myth stylizes Big Sur as a place of paramount exquisiteness, far exceeding the artificial beauties of Kyoto, Amalfi, Cornwall, etc. (the despoiled Old World, Eurasia), on a par with the Tetons and the Grand Canyon. I was not immune to American myth. Since its indigenous cultures more or less succumbed to genocide, there has been popular agreement that the beauty of this continent is its wilderness. I walked into the redwoods. They seemed sized for a lower-gravity life, perhaps on Ganymede. An interpretive sign cited their shallow roots and penchant for capsizing in the first gust of wind as the reason they form groves. Hungry storms, rebuffed, find other targets. Emerging into a warm, bright, breezy meadow thick with butterflies and poppies, I texted him again like a bad poet: "Black oak madrone chervil redwoods poppies everything!!!!!"

As I was falling asleep behind fogged windows in my campsite, he texted back, "Don't miss the oranges (of H. Bosch) ha never read it—not pr0n. only read pr0n. Love you."

———

On the morning of the party I toured Point Lobos, which may be the actual most pretty place in the universe. I mean, say there were a (theistic) God: How would He improve it? What could anybody do to make it any prettier? Every branch of every wind-struck tree had been arranged with perfect gravity to be poetic from all angles. Every rock had fallen with insouciant grace. But it was not habitable. There was nothing edible and insensate growing there, the hallmark of a true paradise. No apple trees, no wild berries, not even a spring of fresh water. Gelatinous seafood edged a chaotic blue ocean where shrieking gulls wheeled above wave-tossed otters. Everywhere I walked, quail dashed away, silent alarm bells quivering on their heads. The park offered perfection to visitors dominated by the visual sense and passive lust for movement—to drivers like me, straight off the highway, plus maybe Futurists and the kind of people who scroll videos on their phones all day. The rushing, heaving feel of the place and the stabbing motion of branches in the wind wore me down. Seeking a quiet corner, I found one under a low bluff, out of the gale, on a beach where a cluster of rocks kept the water smooth enough to let me see fish—petite gray fish, walleyed and impassive as the guardians of Avalon. This beach could be a gateway, I thought. The boat could appear at any moment to take me there.

And suddenly everything was miraculous again. The wind battering the trees above me became a vital element in the composition. There could be no safety without danger, no danger without the glimmer of the festive fairy lights of salvation, drawing one deeper into danger, continually heightening one's sense of enjoying divine protection, an endless spiral . . .

The sublimity of Point Lobos, with its waning and return and teasingly fascist quality, along with my trusting utopian yearnings, made me text Peter one too many times ("you have to come here," "find a way, do it Monday, bring the Italian dude," "super hard to describe") without getting an answer. I stayed for four hours and sent Jay a photo of a jaybird that was hanging around the parking lot.

After leaving Point Lobos, I was in rich-people country, which also reminded me of Jay. Carmel-by-the-Sea was full of cafés where he could have ordered twenty-six dollars' worth of pulled pork and complained about being given too much bread. I found a gas station and bought fresh milk for my Grape-Nuts.

I skipped Monterey—too big—and stopped again at Moss Landing. So placid! RVs inched past the lagoon to park on sugary white sand. Surfers traced curlicues of foam behind surging hordes of sandpipers. I had almost three hours left before I was supposed to show up at the party, and the showers at the public beach in Santa Cruz were less than an hour away. Still I drove on.

The town proved to be Hells Angels top to bottom, as if I had stumbled into a memorial run. Despite the nearly four hundred miles between me and Torrance, I was relieved to see it. I found parking near the beach. The showers were unlocked, and clean enough to use. The water was cold, but not freezing. I washed my hair and scrubbed myself with soap, and no one stole my money. I had used my clean clothes for a pillow, but magically, they were not creased. Good omens, nothing but good omens. I walked out on the pier to let my hair dry while I waited until it was time to go. Little boats and seaborne ducks bobbed on the waves. Dogs and willets stalked the sand. A family with many small children raised a ruckus on the boardwalk. The sun poked warmly through a thin layer of cloud. I texted Peter and got no answer.

The road to the house was steep and winding. About three-quarters of a mile shy of Drew Miller's driveway, the Mazda began to stutter as if it were running out of gas. I shifted into second and then into first. The temperature-warning light came on and a wisp of steam rose from under the hood. I killed the engine and pulled the parking brake as tight as I could, feeling lucky to have started up the hill well ahead of time.

Fifty yards back, I had passed a little wayside by a cluster of mailboxes, so I let the car roll backward and eased it into place, nestled up against a stand of gorse. I grabbed my backpack from the passenger seat to walk the rest of the way.

Miller's mailbox was clearly labeled—no danger of error—and his driveway was a neat, narrow strip of gravel laid over clay, edged on both sides with native brush and fir trees. After a hundred yards I heard a creek flowing to my left. Past it I could see a pasture so large that its gentle curve jutted into the sky like a headland. The pale-green meadow against the blue sky was beautiful in the way I liked best, like the downs of Great Britain—like Glastonbury Tor—swooping, swollen hills of grass, where the trees had been cut down long ago by the Romans or whomever.

Photos of the Marin headlands north of San Francisco made me sad, imagining greedy upstart loggers, but England's sea-level tree line was something I could accept, as if I secretly admired Romans.

I could hear meadowlarks from the open field. The driveway remained in shadow, dipping to cross the creek over a culvert before it hooked off to the right into a hollow filled with redwoods. In this bosky dell, there stood a single car under a homemade red-and-white sign that said PARK HERE. The driveway continued ahead around a curve.

There was no sound. None.

I was thinking, Okay, stay cool, wasn't this supposed to be a party, where are the other people? and starting to sweat, when Peter appeared at the top of a rickety flight of wooden stairs. He was piebald as ever—black hair, white skin—in chinos, a pale-blue button-down, and a loosened crimson Harvard necktie dotted with tiny crimson shields, each bearing the suggestion of an illegibly microscopic silken VERITAS. He descended slowly through the tree trunks, his hand on the railing, staring at me.

"Peter!" I said. "Did you play a trick on me? Is there no party?"

"Yes and no," he said, stepping onto solid ground. "The party doesn't start until seven. But I can't believe how terrific you look. I barely recognized you. Where's your car?"

"It stalled out like fifteen minutes ago, so I walked."

We hugged, and then kissed. Finding my ass was no challenge for him in my new jeans. The backpack made it hard for him to find anything else. I reached inside his shirt from below and behind and felt his moist, slightly hairy back.

"Yasira decided not to come," he said helpfully, untying his tie. "She and her mom are in San Francisco."

"I was thinking maybe there's like a hayloft here somewhere," I said, cutting to the chase like some kind of sex maniac.

"I haven't had time to look around."

"We could just leave. Sneak out, go down to my car, and go to a motel, and come back for the party or something."

"I left my phone in the house. Do you have cash? It'll be at least a hundred dollars, if we can find anything this time on a Saturday. Can you book rooms on your phone?"

Something simple had become inelegant, and I said, "You know what? Forget it. I don't have a credit card, and I need all my cash to get home." That was not quite true, but how could I have sex with him and then take money, even if it was to get home with? Forget it, I would have to kill myself. I knew I had destroyed the mood. I wanted it back. I added, "I'm sorry I said anything."

He had his tie in his hand, like a red flag. He stuffed it in his front pants pocket. We stood still, unsure what to do, hearing a car approach.

Next to where the driveway curved uphill toward the house, a narrower path diverged to follow the course of the stream. He broke the vulgar awkwardness—it felt crushingly eternal until it vanished instantly—by nudging me toward this side trail, up which we uncharacteristically scampered, unwilling to be seen. It wound through the ravine for several hundred yards and dead-ended at a semicircular trickle of waterfall into a shallow pool full of water striders. A Douglas fir three feet in diameter hid a damp niche thick with evergreen needles, where we kneeled facing each other, soon with our shirts up and our pants down.

Eventually we were overwhelmed enough to maneuver into a suggestive position and do something that resembled inter-course in every meaningful regard, especially after I unzipped my boots and got my jeans all the way off. We fucked like champs by virgin standards, sensitively at first, but soon treating our bodies like obstacles we had to push through to unite the flames that were consuming our heads.

I will never forget those moments. Never. When they were over for the time being, I lay reeling in a bewildering mixture of bliss, happiness, enjoyment, contentment, satisfaction, and fulfillment. He kissed me again and again and said that the experience had been too beautiful to believe and that it was time for him to show face because the Italian guy would be waking up from his nap. It was almost half past six. In fantasy novels, time stands still when protagonists sojourn in parallel universes, but in real life it had sped up considerably.

I splashed my underside with water from the freezing creek. He removed bits of crackly foliage and lichen from my hair and watched while I brushed it. He asked whether I was pregnant and I said, "Probably not."

We sought each other's hands and stared into each other's eyes for several seconds, and then we put on our pants and shoes and headed back to the stairs.

After that welcome, I felt a bit quaint, accompanying him to a party full of strangers. But neither of us questioned his duty of punctual attendance.

Eight additional cars were now parked at odd angles under the trees. We could hear voices.

When he got to the top of the stairs, just ahead of me, Peter was almost knocked over by a dog. It looked like a greyhound with extra hair and an even more energetic way of writhing— a Scottish deerhound, maybe, or a super-scruffy borzoi, or an etiolated mutt. I was startled and retreated a few steps back down, but it wanted only to sniff and lick his sticky hands.

"Well, this is Rabelaisian," he said, looking around for a source of water. There was a tap on the side of the house, so he rinsed off, and that seemed to make the dog lose interest.

The stairs terminated at the top of the pasture, with woods at some distance on three sides. Five more cars were parked where the driveway faded into the back lawn. To the west, I could see the ocean.

The house itself looked fresh from a kit, with planed roof beams, cedar shakes still actively warping, and a foundation of jagged stone with wide mortared joints. Each window had twelve or sixteen little panes of glass, a pair of functional green shutters, and a window box with yellow begonias. There were bicycles on the patio, but no toys, and no people visible anywhere.

Peter climbed the stoop and opened the side door, standing aside for me to enter first. The door opened directly into an eat-in kitchen dominated by a table for twenty people. It was one big slab of mahogany that must have weighed half a ton. Along the walls were two stainless-steel refrigerators and an enameled gas stove under a hood as big as a chimney, and from the ceiling over the U-shaped butcher-block island hung dozens of shiny copper pots and silvery sparkling ladles. The shelves were full of Mason jars, cookbooks, and herbs in flowerpots. There were plants and figurines and small appliances and brightly colored dish towels. It was an overstuffed kitchen that could have doubled as a restaurant—plethoric and disorienting.

"Where is everybody?" I said.

"They must be in the front room," Peter said. "Or somewhere outside, or upstairs. The view is better from up there. There's a widow's walk around the roof lantern."

I suggested we take advantage of the situation to eat and

drink without getting in anyone's way. He agreed. He hung his dorky tie over a chair, where we forgot it, never seeing it again. He filled the electric teakettle and turned it on, and we chose peppermint. "I see bagel chips," I said, going to a wall of cabinetry that served as a pantry and taking them down. I sat at the table, ripped open the bag, and raised my eyes to see someone I had not seen in a while: Gautama Buddha in full effect, looking sleepily down at me from a shelf. He was reclining on his right side, as though preparing to die. He was a good three feet long. A narrow sideboard below him was draped in red felt and bore traces of recent sacrifice—flowers, spent incense, a plate of cookies.

My eyes, which had been actively repressing my surroundings, suddenly took note of an irregular pattern of objects formerly inconspicuous among the clutter—a singing bowl, a prayer wheel, a bronze of Avalokiteśvara, a print of Saṃvara doing it with Vajravārāhī.

I put down my stolen chips and said, "This is creepy."

"What's creepy?"

He must have been expecting me to say something about the professional cooking equipment, because he looked perplexed when I asked whether he had noticed all the Buddhist stuff.

"What's wrong with Buddhism?" he asked. "I mean, beyond what's wrong with any religious ideology."

"My mom was a Tibetan Buddhist."

"You had a mother? I thought you were an orphan!"

I had no answer to that. The teakettle boiled. He made us two cups of tea without saying anything. It was apparent that despite all we had shared, we were not intimate friends. I felt the darkness approaching—the fog of banality, the stubborn inadequacy of human life. The metaphysical gravity that tears down beauty, calls love dependence, cannot tolerate complexity.

He put his hand on my shoulder and said, "For fuck's sake, stop thinking and talk to me. Communication oversimplifies things, but thinking is even worse."

I spoke quietly, trying not to leave things out. He sat beside me, watching me intently, alternately touching my hand, my shoulder, my knee, my face. I explained how my father vanished, and that Mom was not Tibetan but from Pasadena. I described her unhappiness, her precipitous flight from Torrance, the basic precepts of her sect, her attachment to her fellow persons of faith, her relationship to the orb, and how she died in poverty, never earning another cent after I was born. I touched on how she had rejected me and how I could not blame her. In conclusion I remarked that I would not be surprised to find that Drew Miller knew her by sight. "Her place was a super-trendy meditation retreat for people from all over the country," I said. "Her Rinpoche was a star."

"He can't possibly need to go on retreats, living here," Peter said, indicating our surroundings with an expansive gesture of his free hand. "Unless he gets distracted by all this stuff? Maybe he has an empty room somewhere, like a carpeted dungeon, with nothing in it but a picture of the Dalai Lama."

"Mom worshiped that guy."

"Anybody would. He was a god-king. The living embodiment of the state, the Mussolini of the Himalayas."

"Isn't he alive?"

"Yeah, but he cast his lot with democracy after the Berlin Wall came down. He's a spiritual leader now. Did you hear he threatened to get back at the Chinese by not reincarnating?

'You can't win, Darth. If you strike me down, I shall become more powerful than you can possibly imagine!' "

We heard a throat-clearing sound—Drew Miller, making his presence known. He was standing in the light by the window at the other end of the table, wearing a brown corduroy blazer, a lean, squirrelly professor with clenched teeth, flushed cheeks, and narrowed eyes.

"Hi, Peter," he said. "I'm glad your guest made it in one piece."

"Yes," Peter said. He stood up, and so did I.

Miller looked me up and down and said, "You could introduce us."

"This is Bran," Peter said, discombobulated. After a pause, he added, "Brandy Thomas, aspiring screenwriter. This is Drew Miller. He writes fiction. Bran's amazing!"

Miller came closer, and we shook hands. "Thanks for coming," he said. Addressing Peter, he added, "Sorry I got a little worked up over what you two were laughing about as I came in. But it was a good test for me. I can be quick to anger sometimes. I was tempted to ask you to leave."

Peter took a clumsy step backward, making a chair leg screech over the terra-cotta floor. He folded his arms and said, "Ask me to leave if you want. But you can't ask Bran to leave. She just drove here from L.A. at your invitation."

"Don't worry," Miller reassured us. "I'm not asking anyone to leave! Please sit down." He pulled out a chair for himself and sat. "Help yourselves to some beer," he said. "And while you're at it"—I guess he thought I had stood up to fetch beer—"could you bring me one, too, Brandy? I'd appreciate it. They're in the left-hand fridge. I'll have an IPA, please."

Moving away, I looked longingly at the door to the outside. Peter was motionless, his eyes fixed on Miller, who leaned back in his chair and looked up at him with the gentle smile of the enlightened preparing to deliver spiritual lessons. My heart sank.

"So I've devoted years of my life to the study of Buddhism," Miller began, "and if there's one thing I've learned, it's that human beings, sweetly pathetic as they are, love to employ delusion to heighten their own suffering. Your false beliefs about Buddhism might come under that heading."

"You're calling me delusional for not subscribing to reincarnation," Peter said.

"Have you ever tried it?"

"Not to my knowledge."

"Would you be open to someone else's knowledge?"

"Please stop," Peter said, defensively raising his open hands. "We're all human beings here. You can patronize me if you want, but not Bran. She had her fill of Buddhism a long time ago, and she's not 'sweetly pathetic.' She's glorious!"

"I admire how you're defending her."

"So you admit 'sweetly pathetic' is an insult, especially for a woman."

"Come on, man," Miller said. "You're the one who came in here and compared Tenzin Gyatso to Mussolini!"

"Should I have compared him to the Ayatollah Khomeini? He was a theocrat. Though he's sweetly pathetic vis-à-vis the Chinese, I'll grant you that!"

Miller shifted his weight, looking at me—I still had not moved, and he clearly wanted beer—and then back at Peter. Miller's face looked hot. Peter looked cooler, but I could smell acrid fear streaming faintly from his armpits.

"Okay," Miller said. "Let's go back to square one. I'm simply asking you, since you're in my home, to treat my spiritual teachers and the tenets of my practice with a little more respect."

"And I'm asking you, since you're in *my universe,* to disregard what you overheard eavesdropping on a private conversation," Peter replied.

Miller bowed his head and muttered something indistinct, and Peter turned to me with panic in his eyes. He looked like all the Kafka characters at once—the land surveyor K. refusing to leave the castle, Josef K. thinking he has to defend himself from the trial, the guy getting his crimes engraved on his back, the beetle that stupidly thinks it should get up and go to work. I tugged on his sleeve, and he lurched sideways and followed me out the door.

I had expected that we would be alone out there, but to my surprise we plunged down the stoop into the middle of a group of party guests that included his Italian. He was at least seventy-five, with the kind of matte pink skin that looks like pressed powder in a compact, wearing a black pinstripe suit and red Pumas. "Peter, Peter!" he cried. "We are going to the sunset! Come with us and bring your beautiful friend! What's your name, beautiful stranger?"

"Bran?" I said. At that moment, I was not entirely sure.

The Italian air-kissed me twice and said, "Lovely, lovely! Now this is a party to remember! Where are you from, my dear? What do you do? You must be an actress!"

"Sometimes," I said. The group slowly moved around the corner of the house, hanging on our every word, because he was the star guest. The evening sky was breathtaking—a slate-gray mass streaked with flame orange, like spilled paint. Peter was still somewhere behind us, processing what he had done. "I'm mostly a screenwriter," I said. "I acted in a couple short films."

"I knew it!" he cried. "It's perfect that you wear green. Diana, the huntress! *Sei stupenda, sei incantevole!* Ah, the sunset! You see those clouds, those short clouds? They are not clouds. They are a kind of flying fish called birds. Zillions of them!" I wanted to ask what kind, but I thought it would be more polite not to, in case he had no idea. Instead, I asked whether he was in the movie industry. "No, no," he said. "I write books. If they adapt my books, fine, but no. I have nothing to do with those monsters. For this I have my agent."

"That's a good idea."

"I give you my agent number."

I smiled and said, "Thank you."

Peter stepped up from behind me and put his hand on my arm. We stayed with the group as it watched the last pink clouds fade. Together we all drifted together up the semicircular front stairway through double doors into a central hallway and then the living room, feeling safety in numbers. The Italian turned his attention somewhere else. Miller was nowhere in sight.

Peter sat down next to me on a love seat and said, "Thanks for saving me. But I sure as hell waded into that one. If this gets back to people, I'm fucked."

"It'll be okay," I said. "He's sworn to loving kindness."

"Thank you for existing," he said. "I mean it. But you get me into trouble. No, I got myself in trouble. I've read his stories. I knew he was a fascist. Why did I even bring you here?—Now I remember. Sorry! For you, I would willingly fuck up everything. I would do it again. It felt good. Even fucking up felt good. What am I saying?"

"That you're chivalrous," I said. "He's a fascist of Avalon, and you're a knight errant of dystopia, and you're fucked, because there's no right life in the wrong one."

We sat watching the others for a while, not touching, like shy strangers who had just met. I was still hungry, so I rose from my seat to go back into the kitchen. It was devoid of people, waiting for the caterer's delivery, but someone had unpacked a bakery display's worth of bread. I ripped off half a naan.

Peter soon followed. We sat down in the same places we had been sitting in before, next to each other at the table, starting over exactly where we had been before Miller came in.

This time Peter had a glass in his hand. "I made myself a whisky," he said. "It's supposed to lower your testosterone levels and cause impotence. I don't think I can get through this night without some impotence. But it tastes like horse manure."

I sniffed it and said, "That's Scotch. It's supposed to taste like peat moss."

He bent to sniff it, and our foreheads met over the melting ice. He said, "It looks better than it tastes. It's a magic crystal ball. I can see your future. Very precise information. HBO is producing *Dystopia* for streaming TV, and you live in Monterey, protected from harm by roving squads of Hells Angels. I hope you're not disappointed. Maybe you were looking for something more vague and oracular."

"Which biker gang controls Cambridge?"

"Pagan's, maybe?"

I recalled that I was not welcome in Cambridge. After a pause I said, "Remind me again why you're marrying that girl."

"Because I can't marry you. We'd break up, and my life

would be the same farcical post-therapeutic wasteland it was before I met you."

There was something rivetingly cruel about what he was saying. But there was also not. I could not help but like his willingness to embrace the anti-Buddhist delusion of selfhood and extend it to no one but me.

I suggested we go outside. We left his whisky on the table and went looking for outbuildings.

The large one I had seen from the air proved to be an old horse barn. Not "old" in the East Coast sense—more like prefab from the seventies, with brown aluminum siding and big sliding doors. We circled it, looking for a door we could open discreetly without making a sound like thunder, and found a small one on the side away from the house. We slipped inside, turned the deadbolt, and looked around in the near-darkness. It had been uninhabited for so long that the horse smell was nearly gone. There was no hay or straw in the loft—none in the entire building, except for a few shreds in the mangers and a scattering of moldering straw on the floors of the two stalls. The only light came from outside, leaking in from Miller's side porch through tiny windows of flyspecked Plexiglas.

We heard scratching and whimpering at the little door. The putative Scottish deerhound had followed us. We let it in, at which point it jumped up on Peter and tried to lick his face. "Someone needs to get this Rabelaisian dog out of my life," he said.

We locked her in the tack room and set about having sex standing up. This is a challenge for anyone, but especially for rank amateurs. By the time we found a kind of groove with my ass on a feed bin, the dog's whining had turned into a thin, coyote-like howl. It was not all that loud. It was not enough to stop us from doing what we were doing. But we should not have been so surprised when Miller let himself into the barn, loudly, via a sliding door.

He went straight to the tack room, not deigning to favor our stooping and scrambling with even a glance. "You people locked up my dog," he said loudly. "I thought he was hurt, or trapped in here with the barn on fire." We were hiding in a box stall by then. He exited the barn with the whimpering, bounding hound, leaving the portal wide open.

Remarking that he was toast, Peter shoved the rattling plywood curtain back into place. His social demise seemed to heighten his sense of sexual liberty and determination to make us both speak in tongues. When we were at last finished with our project, he called me a *"gran pezzo di figliola,"* quoting (he said) the Italian. We kissed a little too much, until we were almost bored of it, and put all our clothes back on.

While we were busy, the clock had made another great leap forward. I said it was high time I left the accursed, yet wonderful party, the memory of which I would cherish as long as I lived. He asked me where my backpack was, and volunteered to retrieve it from the kitchen.

"No, let me get it," I said. "None of these people know me. They're your future colleagues."

"I'm reconsidering trying to work with them," he said. "I'm wondering how many of them haven't heard the story yet. It's been nearly an hour."

"So stay here and wait for me. I'll get my stuff and come right back."

"What if you run into him and he makes a speech?"

We agreed to return to the house together—our third invasion of the kitchen, where we were instantly enveloped by the warmth and hospitality of the future colleagues. They plied us with appetizers of panipuri. There was curry of all kinds on the two stoves. I was ravenous. I found a place at the table to sit and await an entrée. I talked to an English major from Stanford and a creative writing professor from Boulder while Peter, taking a seat opposite, hobnobbed with scholars to his left and right. Miller sat glowering at the head of the table, massaging the dog's ears. I looked at him once—it made me blush—and he got up and left the room.

The rest of the evening passed like a party, the way I always imagined parties, back when I first imagined parties, before I had ever been to one. I ate, talked to strangers, flirted with polite men, heard confessions from charming women, felt happy and pretty and alive.

Evening turned to deepest night, and the party failed to end. An old woman played Elgar on the cello. The lunatic Italian gave me his agent's contact information. A young poet performed their recent work. People queued up favorite dance hits on somebody's smartphone. Conversations moved into the kitchen, upstairs, and out of doors. For a while I talked to Peter over coffee (he made us a pot of coffee) as we moved from room to room. He explained numerous party guests' connections in the academic world. All I remember is how funny it was. He compared himself to Dan Boleyn in *The Apes of God*. Then he talked about me, solemnly, lowering his voice. We danced in a dark corner, touching. He said, "I'm so exhausted, I should lie down," and lay down publicly on a brightly lit couch. Immediately, a drunken scholar sat at his head, inviting him to put it in her lap. He jumped up to get her another drink. I started talking to the carpenter who built the house.

Around five in the morning, when the party was long over, Miller gave me a come-hither smile from a recamier on the other side of an upstairs room, as if he were in a forgiving mood, ready to have a heart-to-heart about my mother, and I decided that it truly was time to go.

I found my backpack under a bench in the kitchen and bid adieu to Avalokiteśvara. I picked my way through the remaining groups of tipsy talkers and stood at the panoramic windows in the front of the house, waiting for Peter to notice I was leaving.

He rose from the sofa where he had been reclining half-asleep, and stood at my side, shading his eyes with both hands to see the full moon over the ocean through the reflective glass. It was setting. The sun was soon to rise behind the mountains.

"You're really going this time," he said.

My heart leapt at his spurious sadness and I said, "Don't fuck with me, Peter!"

I stepped through the archway into the front hall. He followed me, saying, "Listen, Bran. That's what I want to stop doing. Fucking with you. It's over. I'm going to be straight up with you from here on out, forever. Don't go anywhere. Stay with me. In Cambridge. I mean it. I don't know what comes next, but we'll figure something out. I don't care what anybody thinks."

I shook my head and said, "No. I should definitely go."

"I'm embarrassed. I was so stupid. You're not the antithesis of Yasira. You're my one and only. I owe her a major apology. I was using her the whole time, because I was afraid of you."

"And I'm going to leave right now. Because before you told me to stay, you told me I'm really going, and you know how you knew that?" I faced him squarely. "Because you can see the future! You're flying home tonight with her and her mom. That's your plan! And that's how you know I'm really going. Because you have a plan! You're fucking with me, because you know you have time left before you go to the airport. But I'm leaving!"

"I'm going to break off my engagement, Bran."

He had never said it before, and I did not believe it. I said, "No, you're not. That's bullshit."

"I'd text her right now if I weren't so fucking chivalrous. I can't break up with my fiancée by text while she's asleep."

"So call her."

"That's still too shitty. I have to tell her in person. I'd start for San Francisco right now, if I had a car."

"Propose to me, and I'll give you a lift."

"I can't. I'm engaged. And didn't your car break down?"

"So call us a cab."

"There's a limo coming at noon."

"And I'm leaving. Now. I'm out of here."

"Okay, then," he said. "You win. Let's see how far you get." He opened the door.

WEATHER
by Jenny Offill

Lizzie works in the library of a university where she was once a promising graduate student. Her side hustle is answering the letters that come in to Hell and High Water, the doom-laden podcast hosted by her former mentor. At first it suits her, this chance to practice her other calling as an unofficial shrink—but soon Lizzie finds herself struggling to strike the obligatory note of hope in her responses. The reassuring rhythms of her life as a wife and mother begin to falter as her obsession with disaster psychology and people preparing for the end of the world grows. A marvelous feat of compression, a mix of great feeling and wry humor, *Weather* is an electrifying encounter with one of the most gifted writers at work today.

Fiction

A GATE AT THE STAIRS
by Lorrie Moore

Tassie Keltjin, the daughter of a gentleman farmer, has come to a university town as a student. When at twenty she takes a job as a part-time nanny for a mysterious and glamorous family, she finds herself drawn deeper into their world and forever changed. Told through the eyes of this memorable narrator, *A Gate at the Stairs* is a piercing novel of race, class, love, and war in America.

Fiction

THE WOMAN UPSTAIRS
by Claire Messud

Nora Eldridge—elementary schoolteacher, reliable friend and neighbor, repressor of her own artistic and personal dreams—has resigned herself to being on the fringe of other people's achievements. But when a beguiling student enters her classroom, and his glamorous, cosmopolitan parents welcome her into their world, Nora's newfound happiness explodes her boundaries . . . until a subsequent betrayal puts her own sense of self at stake. Claire Messud's masterly novel is the stunning confession of a woman awakened, transformed, and abandoned by a desire for a world beyond her own.

Fiction

VINTAGE BOOKS
Available wherever books are sold.
vintagebooks.com